"This park reminds me of Edinburgh," Connor said. "I would like showing it to you," he added, his fingers entwining with hers.

The innocent statement reminded Leslie that this sudden magic was temporary, that he would soon leave her. It must have reminded him, too, for he impulsively swung her to him, and his lips pressed hard against hers with kind of desperation.

The world seemed to erupt in a giant field of flame. If he hadn't been holding her close, she might have fallen. There was so much strength in his body, so much heat, so much harsh longing. She felt his lips search for a response, and the kiss deepened as her mouth opened and welcomed him. His hands caressed her tenderly, searching rather than demanding, promising rather than taking. She didn't care that this was a public park, that anyone might come along. Connor MacLaren made her feel alive again. . . .

WHAT ARE *LOVESWEPT* ROMANCES?

They are stories of true romance and touching emotion. We believe those two very important ingredients are constants in our highly sensual and very believable stories in the *LOVESWEPT* line. Our goal is to give you, the reader, stories of consistently high quality that may sometimes make you laugh, sometimes make you cry, but are always fresh and creative and contain many delightful surprises within their pages.

Most romance fans read an enormous number of books. Those they truly love, they keep. Others may be traded with friends and soon forgotten. We hope that each *LOVESWEPT* romance will be a treasure—a "keeper." We will always try to publish

LOVE STORIES YOU'LL NEVER FORGET
BY AUTHORS YOU'LL ALWAYS REMEMBER

The Editors

Loveswept ® 602

Patricia Potter
Troubadour

BANTAM BOOKS
NEW YORK · TORONTO · LONDON · SYDNEY · AUCKLAND

TROUBADOUR

A Bantam Book / March 1993

*If you would be interested in receiving protective vinyl
covers for your Loveswept books, please write to this address
for information:*

*Loveswept
Bantam Books
P.O. Box 985
Hicksville, NY 11802*

ISBN 0-553-44369-0

Published simultaneously in the United States and Canada

PRINTED IN THE UNITED STATES OF AMERICA

OPM   0 9 8 7 6 5 4 3 2 1

One

Leslie Turner eyed the arriving passengers as if searching out a snake in a woodpile.

And she had a number of unkind feelings for Gillian Collins, her partner in their public-relations firm, the Word Shop, who had gone out of town, dumping her newest client on Leslie.

To add insult to injury, the new client was the one creature in the world that Leslie loathed on general principle: A musician. Never mind that he was a folk musician, not a rock star, as Leslie's late husband had been. Musicians were all alike. God knew she'd seen enough of them.

The plane had been several minutes late, and Leslie had even uncharitably hoped it had disappeared over the Bermuda Triangle. But seconds later came an announcement that the plane was arriving. No reprieve, after all.

Damn, Leslie thought. A musician. A Scot. And she had to play nursemaid. But the Word Shop had already accepted the hefty retainer sent by a New York public-relations agency to arrange local appearances and interviews. At least the check had been large enough to give the firm the financial cushion it needed.

Her hand tensed around the sign she was carrying, which she'd written herself. It simply said MACLAREN. She had been in no mood to make it fancier, nor did she intend to be more than coldly polite for the next few days.

Connor MacLaren. Leslie had paid scant attention when Gillian had talked about him, except for the size of the fee. What did a folksinger look like? Leslie wondered as she continued to search faces.

But then she had to wonder no longer. Even if she hadn't ever seen a Connor MacLaren, she knew she was seeing one now. And the impact was like a sledgehammer in her stomach.

Standing several inches over six feet, with vivid blue eyes and black hair peppered with white, he was one of the most striking men she'd ever encountered, and his attire set off his dark good looks perfectly.

He was wearing a bluish-gray tailored jacket over a cream-colored linen shirt that opened in a split at the neck. The shirt was clasped by a heavy leather belt around a lean waist, which led her eyes down to a green-and-blue-plaid kilt that ended at the knees of the most sinewy pair of legs she'd ever seen. Stockings that reached almost to the knee did nothing to hide the strength in those legs, and Leslie was stunned by the pure, raw, almost primitive masculinity of the costume.

Very briefly—no, not so briefly—came a forbidden thought: Was it true Scotsmen wore nothing under their kilts? A shiver suddenly ran down her spine. A most unwelcome shiver.

Leslie silently cursed her absent partner again, and then herself. Maybe Gillian was right. She had been far too long without a man. Her eyes moved upward. Beneath the kilt and shirt was clearly a hard, lean body. A pair of very bright, very warm eyes viewed her and her handwritten sign from under dark bushy eyebrows arched in a question mark.

It was as if a streak of bright blue electricity had struck her, and the cardboard started to fall from hands suddenly gone numb. Although holding a guitar case and garment bag, the object of her sudden confusion was quick to rearrange his burden and reach for the cardboard before it hit the floor.

Her gaze followed the kilt's movement as it moved against an enticingly masculine body. When he straightened, a slight smile on his lips, she felt like a complete idiot.

"Gillian?"

Only easygoing Gillian would encourage clients she'd never met to call her by her first name.

Leslie shook her head. "I'm Leslie Turner, Gillian's partner. She . . . had an emergency."

"Ah," he said, "you donna look like I pictured her."

He was disappointed, no doubt, Leslie thought. Gillian flirted with her voice, which was low and husky and sexy, with a hint of the exotic, while Leslie was always the professional. Today she had dressed conservatively in a severely tailored suit and blouse. She'd chosen the outfit because she wanted to feel every bit the self-assured, self-sufficient woman she'd become, but all of a sudden what she felt was every minute of her thirty-seven years.

"And you are very kind tae meet me," he added, as his gaze slid over her. There was a thick burr in his deep voice, and the words rolled off his tongue like a song. He regarded the sign in his hand for a moment, and then dumped it in a nearby trash can. "Purrrrpose fulfilled," he said, grinning, "unless you think you might be picking up another Connor MacLaren someday."

His good-natured humor was disarming. Or it

would have been disarming if she hadn't had prior experience with performers, Leslie thought perversely. Nonetheless, she wasn't able to repress even the slightest smile at his words. There couldn't be another Connor MacLaren in the wide world.

Lord, she hoped not, as she felt his Scottish charm begin to drain her hostility like water through a colander. She fought to regain it. She knew the superficiality of charm. Yet there was a warmth in his eyes that was almost spellbinding. What else would explain her lapse of speech, her sudden awkwardness?

He shifted his load and set his guitar case down on the floor. Then he stretched out his hand to her, requiring her to do the same.

They clasped hands, his large one over her small one, and a shock ran through her again. But this was more than that first blinding flash of lightning. This touch sent ripples of unfamiliar sensation through her. She met his gaze, feeling a growing tension deep within her. He had a marvelous face, strong and distinctive, with laugh lines traveling from eyes that were topped by black bushy brows. Sensuous was the only word for his mouth; the lips firm but wide, the corners curling upward in a mischievous twist. And a very attractive cleft indented a strong chin.

He was devastating.

Leslie jerked her hand away as if burned, and she sensed his surprise. No doubt he was accustomed to fawning women.

Just like Tommy Turner.

"We'd best hurry," she said, looking down at her watch. "You have an interview in an hour. I have your complete schedule. You can look at it in the car." She purposely made her voice cool, without a hint of the cordiality that usually lurked there. It was self-defense, pure and simple.

He tipped his head slightly, as if trying to analyze

her hostility, but his words, when they came, were all business, even if accompanied by a slightly baffled smile. "Gillian . . . Miss Collins . . . said she ha' scheduled a number of interviews."

Leslie nodded, trying to keep her expression impersonal even as she saw any number of women's eyes turning enviously in their direction. "She's arranged interviews with four television and radio stations, several cable stations, and a number of newspapers."

"And you're going tae be my shepherd . . . shepherdess?"

It took Leslie a moment to translate the "tae" to "to." She swallowed hard from the combined effect of charm, a face women would kill for, and a soft Scottish brogue that was in itself spellbinding. "Until Gillian returns," she finally managed.

"Guid," he said, and Leslie had to mentally translate the word into "good." He grinned. "I believe myself in very efficient hands." The *r* in "very" rolled in the air. She wished it didn't sound so damned . . . mesmerizing.

Leslie steeled herself. Why did he have to be so attractive? Her eyes fell to the guitar case, and that object strengthened her protective core. How well she remembered another guitar. It had been her competition, along with drugs, alcohol, and groupies.

She met his eyes, but only with the greatest of willpower. "The interview I mentioned . . . it's their only opening this week, and we should be there in an hour."

He looked at her quizzically. "And wha' if the plane had been late?"

"We would have missed a great opportunity," Leslie said. "I was supposed to call if you were late, and the station would have used a taped segment." She didn't add how much she'd wished he *would* be late, perhaps even lost forever, but from his slight grin she guessed he had some idea about her thoughts.

"Aye, lass," he said. "But I'm here and yours tae command."

The image those words created made her shiver again, even though she doubted every word that came from his mouth. She turned without saying more, but her legs moved quicker than usual to the underground people-mover that linked the concourses of the huge airport. She and the folk-singer squeezed into an already packed car, forcing an intimacy between them that did nothing for her state of mind. Pressed against his hard, solid body, she felt suddenly aflame with awareness. Even his breath floated down to touch her ear, and the smell of his musky cologne was intoxicating.

The car lurched forward, and she was thrown backward. As she felt one of Connor MacLaren's arms go around her and right her, her blood ran faster. It didn't help to realize that he had rattled her so much, she hadn't grabbed the pole that was there just to prevent such a predicament.

"I think I like this train," he said in a sexy whisper that she hoped no one else could hear. She reached out for the pole now and hung on for dear life. Never in her ten years in this business had she felt this kind of reaction to a client. *Gillian's client,* she reminded herself.

When the train jerked to a stop a few minutes later, his strong arm tightened again around her, steadying her, and Leslie felt a rush of heat surge through her body.

"All right, lass?" he said in that deep burr.

She had never been called "lass" before. She decided she liked the sound of it, and then mentally scolded herself. But when she looked up to answer him, her words stopped in her throat. The top of her head came only to his chin, and her gaze was just millimeters away from the path of bronze skin revealed by the open V of his shirt. Struck speechless, she could only nod. *Heavens above, six days with this man, three of them nearly round the clock.* When the doors opened, she practically bolted outside, never turning to determine whether or not he was following her.

They made the baggage area in record time, far too quickly for even the first bags to have arrived, and she was forced to stand with him, waiting. He looked both puzzled and amused by her speed, but his eyes were friendly. Friendly as a python, she thought, as it wrapped itself around you before squeezing you to death. Tommy had almost done that to her. She had vowed no one would ever have that chance again.

"You've been to Atlanta before?" She tried small talk. Anything to take her attention from those eyes that regarded her so frankly and with such . . . interest.

"Only the airport. I found you canna go much anywhere withou' going through your airport. But I always wanted tae stay awhile. Now I know why." The accent was more distinctive than ever, and the implication of his words crawled into Leslie's consciousness, settling there like a snifter of fine brandy, glowing and comforting.

Damn him.

Almost automatically, Leslie chanted, "Whether going to heaven or hell, you still have to go through Atlanta."

"I hope no' to test the latter," he replied.

Leslie found herself raising an eyebrow in disbelief.

"I see a wee bit of doubt there. You'll have tae tell me why."

Leslie forced her gaze away and toward the baggage carousel, which was now beginning to churn out luggage.

"Later then," he said with a challenge. "And would you mind now watching the guitar while I fetch the rest?"

She nodded as he set the case down next to her and then moved forward, mixing with the crowd gathering around the incoming baggage. He showed no impatience but stood relaxed, accepting curious glances with an amiable nod of his head. His back was to her, and she could look with impunity now. Maddeningly, this side of him was almost as attractive as the front, the kilt hugging his lean hips to advantage, the jacket stretching over broad shoulders, the dark tousled hair curling around his neck. Her fingers suddenly itched to feel it.

Down, girl, she told herself. But still she couldn't take her eyes away from him, from the clothes that gave him an aura of old-world virility.

He was not at all what she had anticipated. She'd expected him to be young and arrogant, as so many of Gillian's clients were. Shallow and thoughtless. He was, she guessed, somewhere in his mid-forties. There was an energy and magnetism about him that made him ageless, and yet the small lines around his eyes and the sprinkling of white in that thick hair spoke of experience. And there was no hint of arrogance about him, only a captivating personal warmth. But it was probably just the kind of warmth so many successful entertainers cultivated, she warned herself. They had to have it to succeed, and she had discovered that most of them spread it around freely. Very freely.

Leslie didn't want to like him, couldn't afford to like him. It was disconcerting that she did. Or was it simply that musicians had a fatal attraction for her? She turned her still-simmering frustration against Gillian on herself.

She would have to be extremely careful not to let her feelings go beyond a distant professionalism.

Besides, she assured herself, she was not the type of woman who would appeal to a man like Connor MacLaren, who quite obviously could have anyone he wanted. He was probably married with children and had women in every city he visited.

She wished now she had listened more closely to Gillian's ramblings, and that she'd read Connor's press release more carefully. She had copies of it in the car, ready to hand out at their stops. But she had been in a hurry, her resentment had been boiling, and she had not really wanted to know more than what she had to.

She still didn't want to know more, she told herself. He was just a client.

He turned, a much-battered piece of luggage in his hand as well as the garment bag, and she couldn't help but admire the lithe grace of that strong body. He carried himself with assuredness and confidence, and yet with a spring in his step as if ready to embrace whatever he encountered, despite what must have been an exhausting flight from Scotland.

He leaned over to take the guitar, but to her own surprise, Leslie found herself snatching it up instead.

"I can manage," he said. "I've become quite guid at this."

Telling herself she was only compensating for her somewhat surly welcome, Leslie found herself smiling up at him and saw his answering smile. There was the darnedest twinkle in his eyes.

"I'm used to carrying guitars," she said. She tried to analyze his charm. Was it like Tommy's, as easy to turn off as it was to turn on? The thought broke her smile. "We'd better hurry," she added, her voice unsteady. "Remember the interview." She started walking quickly, giving him no choice but to follow.

But then he was striding along with her, a low chuckle making her slow her steps slightly.

"You'd make a good drum major," he murmured. "Such a waste . . ."

She glanced up, but he merely raised his dark brows. She felt a delicious tingle run up her backbone. Something about him promised magic.

But she didn't believe in magic.

She didn't believe in performers.

And she certainly didn't believe in love.

It was, she suddenly realized, going to be a very long week.

Connor followed Leslie's quick, efficient steps, watching her straight, stiff back and wondering at the conflicting signals he was catching from her.

He was tired, yet his encounter with Leslie Turner had been invigorating. And disconcerting. It had been a long time since he'd felt this stirring deep inside. He shook his head to rid it of distractions. This was his first stop on a four-month tour of the United States, and he always looked forward to his appearances in the country. Here in Atlanta he would be featured at the annual Stone Mountain Highland Games and Scottish Festival, an event he particularly enjoyed. The audiences at the Scottish festivals around the country were always receptive, hungry for the kind of music he loved to play.

The touring season also took his mind from the loneliness he often felt in the house in Edinburgh, which held so many memories, so much pain. Again he shook his head to whisk those thoughts aside.

He had looked forward to meeting Gillian Collins. He had liked her voice on the telephone, the spontaneous enthusiasm in it, and had felt a sudden rapport with her. Somehow he had known, the moment he had stepped off the plane, that the woman waiting for him was not Gillian.

The replacement had not been a disappointment, however, despite his feeling that Leslie Turner was not altogether welcoming and quite obviously did not share Gillian's enthusiasm for him.

There was something extremely appealing about Leslie, and he had felt an unusual jarring inside when his fingers had touched hers. She was very pretty in a quiet, almost serene way. She wore her hair short, and it was a lovely color, auburn with touches of gold. Her eyes were a cloudy gray-green, like the ocean that quietly lapped Scotland's shores. But there had been nothing calm about her eyes ever since he'd stepped off the plane. They had flashed with strong emotion, and he found himself fascinated with what he'd glimpsed there: Fire and ice, passion and control.

They stopped for a guard who checked his luggage tags against his claim check. He was very conscious of many eyes on him, as there always were when he wore the kilt. He'd known there was an interview scheduled shortly after his arrival, and he hadn't been sure how much time he would have to change; television interviewers always loved the kilt.

They walked out into the bright sunlight of a Southern fall day, his companion's stride still doing shame to a Highlander's forced march. She stopped at a sensible four-door medium-size green-gray sedan. He wondered briefly if she would be any more communicative when trapped inside with him. He suddenly liked the idea—liked it, in fact, very much.

His luggage stored inside the trunk, he nearly had to leap around to open the driver's door for her, and then hurried around to his own door, keeping in his mind the brief smile she had given him. But once inside the car, he found a sheaf of papers more or less shoved at him.

He placed them in his lap without looking at them. "Tell me about the first interview," he said, forcing her to meet his gaze before she started the car.

"It's all in there," she told him. "Gillian is very thorough."

"But I would like tae know what Leslie Turner thinks."

"Leslie Turner thinks you will do just fine," she said. "It's a segment with Jan Carroll on the noon news. She's very easygoing and glib. You should suit."

"Glib," he repeated. "I'm not quite sure how you mean tha'."

"Personable," she amended, realizing that some of her disapproval was revealing itself. She hadn't meant it to. She had merely wanted to be professional. Aloof.

How could she be aloof in the car with him? She had always thought the sedan was a good size before. Now, it seemed like a midget model, and Connor MacLaren a giant, filling the interior with the masculine scent of his cologne and the raw vitality he exuded. Her eyes were locked to his questioning ones, and he was leaning forward, toward her till she felt like a puppet being drawn closer and closer. She wondered how his lips would feel against her face, her lips. . . .

Dear God, what was happening to her? She jammed the key into the ignition, started the car, and shifted to reverse. The car jerked backward, just barely missing another car. Her thoughts were suddenly in a jumble, her mind not responding to any of its ordinary stimuli—but to others quite provoking.

Drive, she directed herself. And try not to kill yourself or him. Robin still needs you, and probably someone needs him too. The thought was somehow painful.

"Read," she ordered. "And then we'll talk."

"Whatever you say, lass," her passenger said with equanimity.

But when she had to wait in line to pay the parking fee, she turned, almost against her will, and saw he wasn't reading at all. Instead, he was perusing her in a very unprofessional way. She wasn't at all aware that she was staring back until she heard a honking behind her and looked ahead. Two cars had passed through the cashier and exit gate in front, and she hadn't even noticed.

"Damn," she whispered again, remembering she'd started the day that way. She was beginning to suspect her language was not going to improve anytime soon.

Two

Leslie confined her wayward thoughts in a mental box, as she had learned to do years ago, concentrating solely on driving and trying to block out the masculine energy simmering next to her.

She also tried to avoid looking down . . . at the masculine leg that almost met her own leg. He had moved closer to the center of the seat, and she sensed that he was still gazing at her. Though for the life of her, she didn't know why.

Leslie had never been overly pleased with her looks. Her mouth was too wide, her chin too stubborn, her coloring rather muted even with the auburn hair. Its color was subdued, more brown than red.

And whatever confidence, or illusions, she'd once had about her appearance had been thoroughly destroyed by Tommy, who'd told her, on the day he'd left for good, that she could never hold a man.

"You said Gillian . . . Miss Collins . . . ha' an emergency. Nothing bad, I hope."

His voice, low and concerned and rhythmic, was seductive in itself. It also carried a measure of concern.

Leslie thought of Gillian's emergency and had to smile. "No, not unless you call a stranded Russian circus bad."

There was a silence, and Leslie was pleased she had finally disconcerted him. "A Russian Circus?" The words were almost choked, whether by surprise or humor, she couldn't tell.

She grinned, unable to stop the retort. "I'm afraid you were bumped by some horses, dogs, and a chimpanzee. Gilly decided to be their champion and go to their rescue."

"A chimpanzee?"

"I'm afraid so," she repeated sorrowfully.

"Ouch," he said, but without resentment, only a humorous fatalism. "I've been rejected before, but never for a monkey."

"I'm afraid Gillian sometimes gets . . . an enthusiasm, and now it's saving a Russian circus stranded here by its backers. The animals were impounded in Boston, and she believes she can get them freed."

"I'll remember that if I ever get impounded," Connor said, chuckling.

Leslie couldn't suppress a smile, but then a car darted in front of hers, and she gratefully returned her attention back to the road. Still, she wanted to keep looking at Connor, and listening to that voice.

"And you and . . . Gillian are partners?"

"In the Word Shop," Leslie explained. "We do public relations and advertising, all kinds. Gillian specializes in entertainment."

"And you?"

"Real estate . . . business."

There was a brief silence as he digested the information. She heard his dry amusement when he finally spoke. "And you were shanghaied into fetching a wayward troubadour?"

That was just about it, Leslie thought wryly,

disconcerted at his insight. "Something like that," she admitted, trying to keep her mind and eyes on the road.

"I will try tae behave myself," he said, the burr seeming to echo in the interior of the car. "I think," he added carefully.

The taunt was a challenge, plain and simple, and Leslie's insides, already shaken by her physical reactions to him, turned over again. She shook her head and concentrated on the freeway into Atlanta, which did, thank God, demand her full attention. She whizzed along with the most venturesome of the drivers, going a little faster than usual.

Connor glanced at the papers she'd given him, absorbed what information was there, and then turned his attention back to her. He thoroughly enjoyed looking at her, content as he watched many different expressions flit across her face. Bemusement as they'd left the parking lot, then a kind of self-anger, and then concentration.

"You're a very good driver," he observed aloud.

"Thanks," she said in a clipped voice that didn't invite additional comment. He ignored the warning.

"You were born here?"

Leslie felt everything in her tighten up. Feeling flooded by the old shyness she'd thought she'd learned to cover up, she nodded.

"You've lived here all your life?"

She allowed herself a glance at him. It was a mistake. His eyes were twinkling, and she realized that he enjoyed trying to make her talk. She sighed. "Yes, Mr. MacLaren, and yourself?"

"We Scots pretty much stay in one place. I was born in Edinburgh and still live there. But I know Americans are different."

"Americans," she said a little sharply, "are probably like Scots . . . all different."

"Aye, I stand corrected, Miss Turner. Some, though, are much bonnier than others."

"And some Scots are more . . ." She searched for a word suitable for a paying client.

"Challenging?"

"That's not exactly what I was thinking of."

"Is it Scots you object tae?" he asked abruptly. "Or folksingers?"

"Musicians," she admitted suddenly, wondering why the word popped out of her mouth. She was mortified that her feelings had been so obvious, but at the same time she hoped it would end the discussion.

"All musicians?"

"Yes."

"You said at the airport you were used tae carrying guitar cases," he noted.

"Yes," she said in a tone that implied she was going to say no more.

Leslie felt a sudden stab of guilt. She had been far less than courteous, which was totally unlike her. But he did such strange things to her equilibrium, and that hadn't happened to her in years, not since she'd taken control of her life. Now, she felt that control assaulted, and it frightened her. She didn't like the effect of his voice on her, or his touch, or even his gaze.

She bit her lip and tried to make amends of a sort. "I hope you'll enjoy your stay in Atlanta."

"I plan tae," he said lazily, not pressing his earlier question. And from the corner of her eye she watched him stretch and lean back like a large jungle cat after a good meal.

Leslie didn't intend to be his meal and, giving herself a brief warning, turned all her attention back to the road.

They arrived at the television station thirty minutes ahead of time, something of a record from the airport. Leslie quickly opened her own door and descended, her medium heeled shoes making staccato sounds on the pavement as she made her way toward the building.

"Ms. Turner!"

She turned and saw he was waiting at the rear of the car.

"My guitar."

She returned, feeling foolish as she unlocked the trunk and watched him pull out the instrument. He then took off his jacket and replaced it with a black leather vest from his garment bag. He looked now like a breath-stoppingly handsome, devil-may-care rogue who'd just stepped out of the past.

"My uniform," he explained with a slightly abashed look that was completely beguiling. He laid the jacket he had been wearing on the garment bag and shut the trunk.

"Now, lass, let's go and conquer the Philistines," he said, picking up his guitar case.

"Philistines?"

"Those poor souls who haven't yet discovered the riches of Scottish music," he said with mock despair as he shook his head with obvious sympathy for those so deprived.

The interior of the reception area was elegant and showy, presided over by a very pretty girl whose eyes widened when she saw Connor MacLaren swagger through the doors.

Leslie immediately scolded herself for being unfair. Connor MacLaren did not swagger. She wished he did. Tommy had swaggered. He had made swaggering into an art form.

But Connor MacLaren did nothing of the kind. His steps were too forceful, too sure. Leslie realized that confidence must have something to do with it. Tommy's swaggering covered his raging insecurities, but she hadn't realized that until years later, when so much damage had already been done.

She hated the memories that came back, and they did nothing to endear Connor MacLaren to her. Connor MacLaren. Her responsibility for a week. Her package. Yes, she must think of him as nothing but a plain package.

Her gaze went to him, and she saw that he was patiently awaiting her next action. Darn it. He was anything but a plain package—more like one filled with dynamite. She couldn't help a rueful smile from spreading across her face.

"You ha' a very bonny smile," he said, as if they were alone and not standing in front of a fascinated young lady whose lacquered nails rested on a large ledger that she held open for them to sign.

And you have one that lures even the angels into Hades, she thought. But she reassembled her defenses and merely said, "Thank you," before turning to the receptionist. "Connor MacLaren. He has an interview with Jan Carroll."

The girl stared at Connor for several seconds before pushing the book and a pen forward, the pen dropping from her hand as he winked at her. "Are all the lasses in Atlanta so pretty?"

Leslie gritted her teeth as her heart lurched. It had been anchored in place for eighteen years, and she wasn't going to let anyone play with it again. Yet disappointment seeped into her. He had tossed out the compliment so easily, and its very adroitness dissipated the reluctant pleasure she had felt just seconds earlier when he'd remarked on her smile.

"Let's go," she said curtly. "We're running a little late." She moved toward the stairs that led to the studios, not wanting to witness more of his flirtation with the receptionist.

What was wrong with her?

She felt his presence beside her, and then his

hand touched her elbow in a courteous yet almost possessive way. Even through the material of her suit jacket, his hand seemed to burn her.

"This way," she said without turning toward him, for she was afraid if she did, her step might falter. They came to another reception area, this one full of people scurrying around.

Jan Carroll was there waiting for them, obviously alerted from downstairs to their arrival. "You must be Connor," she said, not waiting for introductions. "I've been expecting you. Let's go."

Connor looked at Leslie with a question in his eyes.

"I'll wait out here," she said.

"I'm grateful for your care," he told her.

"You're going to be great," Jan commented as her eyes evaluated him from head to toe, and then lingered on the guitar. "Will you sing?"

"If you have time."

"Oh, I'll make time," she said. Her eyes sort of glazed over, just as the receptionist's had. "We'd better hurry."

Leslie sat in front of the glass separating the small guest area from the soundstage. This was an hour show, the first thirty minutes devoted entirely to news and the second to features and happenings in the city.

The news time was, as usual, depressing.

Murder, mayhem, and natural disasters were today's topics, which was, perhaps, why the appearance of a relaxed Connor MacLaren seated in a chair next to Jan's was comforting. His magnetism and energy transmitted itself through the glass and even from the television screen that was in the room.

As she'd waited for his appearance, Leslie had taken the opportunity to read the bio Gillian had prepared, and she was a little surprised at the brevity of it. Gillian was usually more thorough, but this said nothing about family, only that Connor MacLaren belonged to the MacLaren clan in Scotland, was forty-two years old, and that he'd been a professional singer for nearly thirty of those years. This would be his sixth tour of the United States. He had six albums to his credit.

Leslie had noticed he was not wearing a wedding ring, but then, Tommy hadn't either. It "ruined" his image, he said, and Leslie supposed that MacLaren used the same reasoning.

So now she listened intently as Jan probed gently. "You've been performing professionally since you were twelve?"

"Aye," he said. "My brother was a singer, and he taught me. We used tae perform together." Connor grinned, a suddenly boyish smile that seemed to embrace the entire television audience. "He grew out of it, but I never did. There's something about traveling around the world that appeals tae the Scottish adventurer in me."

"Are Scots adventurers?" Jan asked.

"Aye," he said again. "We've scattered ourselves around the world, which is why there are so many Scottish festivals now. Germany. Indonesia. Even Japan. And especially America and Canada. We settled much of America, you know. Your Appalachians ha' especially strong Scottish ties. And there's a strong hunger among these people for a taste of their heritage."

"They say everyone's an Irishman on Saint Patrick's Day. Do you sometimes think it's the same for Scots when there's a Scottish festival?"

"The Scots know how tae hold a party. It's all a myth, you know, about us being dour folk," he answered with mischief.

"And you will be singing . . . ?"

"Thursday night at the Tattoo, and again on

Friday at the hotel, and then every few hours at the festival."

"Tattoo?"

"Ah it's one of the grandest Scottish parties of all," he said. "Pipes and drums and brass bands from all over the world. They gather taegether tae play their music and march. It's a grand sight, tae see four or five hundred musicians, all in different plaids, producing splendid sounds. The Atlanta Tattoo is one of the largest and finest in the world."

"Perhaps we can have a taste of what's in store."

"Aye, it would be my pleasure," Connor said with that glorious rolling voice. He reached down and opened the guitar case, taking out the instrument with almost reverent hands.

"This is one of our favorite Scottish melodies, the 'Skye Boat Song.' It tells the story of the escape of Bonnie Prince Charlie from the English after the Battle of Culloden. His followers massacred and his kingdom lost, he's fleeing tae the Island of Skye." Connor's fingers lovingly skimmed the strings of the guitar, sounding the first plaintive notes, then following with a deep, mellow baritone voice that conveyed the tragic sorrow of the defeated would-be king.

Totally absorbed, Leslie heard the grief of a young prince fleeing his country in Connor MacLaren's voice, the echoes of a war-torn nation, and she felt an emotional intensity and empathy that was so strong, she could hardly bear it.

Her gaze went to his, and she saw that he was looking toward her, not the camera, and then his face turned again to sing directly to the audience, the last haunting notes of the song echoing in the studio.

There was silence for a moment, and then Jan gushed, "Where do we get tickets?"

Leslie didn't listen to the rest. Jan and Connor

would conclude by talking about the Scottish Festival, and Leslie needed air. Air and distance. She almost stumbled out the door and then leaned against the wall.

Such strong attraction at first sight—was it simply lust? These things didn't happen. At least, they didn't happen to Leslie Turner, who had already learned her lesson. Never had she responded to anyone like this, not even to Tommy, whom she once thought she loved with all her heart.

Tommy had been nothing like Connor MacLaren. Her husband's music had been hard rock. He'd also played a guitar, but not one that sang sweetly; one that was amplified and pounded out rhythm. She still remembered that rhythm, which had taken her young husband to the heights of success for such a brief time. If it had not been for the drugs . . .

But then, if not drugs, it might well have been something else. Tommy hadn't been able to handle success; it had come too quickly. It was the classic case of too much, too soon.

"There you are. . . ."

The baritone voice that had been singing about Scotland's past now startled her from her own.

She turned. He had rolled up his sleeves, and the vest was untied. He looked compellingly masculine. She wasn't sure she wanted compellingly masculine company at the moment.

"You were very good," she said honestly.

"That's why you left?" he observed with dry humor.

"I didn't," she denied, embarrassed. "Not until you finished."

"You don't have tae take me tae the hotel, Ms. Turner," he said, and she understood that her resentment had been obvious. "I'm a big lad, and I can take a cab."

"I want to," she replied, finding she meant it. She liked him, and she liked his music despite all her attempts to do otherwise. She suddenly realized exactly how unfair she had been. "Really," she added, "and please call me Leslie."

His eyes seemed to penetrate straight through to her soul as if testing her sincerity, and she felt ashamed of herself. Never in her life had she been as ungracious as she had this morning. She couldn't blame it all on memories that, once revived, didn't want to go away.

"Please," she added.

Connor nodded, a smile creasing his face and crinkling the area around his eyes. "Let's go," he said.

She talked during the trip to the hotel, giving a brief history of Atlanta and discussing the various interviews that had been arranged. Enthusiasm had crept into her voice because she knew now how well he would do with all of them.

There was nothing arranged tonight. Gillian had thought he would need some rest after the long flight and time change. As they drove up to the hotel, Leslie told him she would pick him up at eight the next morning.

He didn't move from the seat. Instead, he took her left hand and looked at it. "No ring," he observed. "And I hate tae eat alone. Would you join me?"

She was surprised how much she wanted to accept the invitation. But she had told Robin she would be home tonight.

"I'm sorry," she said. "My daughter expects me."

Disappointment flickered across his face, and her regret deepened. It must be dispiriting to travel so far and then end up alone in a hotel. Empathy overcame her, even as she realized it was probably a terrible mistake.

"Would you like to take potluck at my house?"

"Potluck?"

"Anything that's in the refrigerator," she explained.

"That sounds like an adventure, but I donna want tae impose. I've already taken up tae much of your day."

"As long as you don't expect much, or mind endless questions from a seventeen-year-old."

"Seventeen?" Surprise was in the question, and Leslie couldn't help but feel pleasure wash over her.

"Going on thirty," she quipped, unexpectedly at ease with him.

"Do I have time tae change?"

"What about time to rest?" Leslie said. "I should go back to the office, and I'll pick you up at five."

He hesitated. "Are you sure now, lass?"

Leslie hadn't been at all sure about the invitation. But suddenly she was. She didn't know whether it was the "lass" that did it, or the honest concern in his voice, but she wanted him to come. Badly.

She tried to justify her reaction. He was, after all, a client, and he would be here only a week. Other performers and dignitaries would be pouring into town tomorrow for the festival, and his time would be taken. One evening, particularly with her daughter present, wasn't too much to offer a client, a well-paying client at that.

"If you bring your guitar. I think my daughter would enjoy it, and I'm trying to wean her from heavy metal."

"I'm not sure I can compete with that." Connor grinned. "But it would be a pleasure," he said formally. "I donna get much home-cooked food."

He must mean on the tours, Leslie thought. Connor MacLaren had to be married. No one so attractive could have existed forty-two years without getting married.

"How long is this tour?" She suddenly didn't want him to leave the car, didn't want to lose that uncommonly attractive brogue of his.

"Four months. From here I go to Knoxville, and then tae Memphis, Chicago, San Francisco, and up the Pacific Coast. I'll end up in New York."

"And then?" she asked, wondering where he made his home—and with whom.

"Home tae Edinburgh," he said.

"And your family? Don't they miss you?"

The light went from his eyes, and his jaw seemed to stiffen. "There is no one now, except my brother. And his family."

Leslie couldn't explain the sudden relief she felt. She shouldn't. She would feel much safer if he were married and had a horde of children. But she knew he wasn't lying. There had been pain in his brief reply, pain that was still alive. It had clouded the blue eyes that were usually so incredibly vivid.

But then the cloud was gone, and she wondered if she imagined it as he opened his car door.

"If I can have your keys," he said, "I'll get my luggage."

Leslie had been ready to spring out to open the trunk herself, but she let him do it. She was confused, thinking ahead to tonight and what she would prepare for the meal. She never had dinner parties, and she usually made spaghetti when Gillian or another friend came over for supper. She tried to share a meal with Robin each night, but often it was only a hamburger and salad or a casserole, and they frequently ate out since Leslie often worked late.

But there was more than food to worry about. Leslie hadn't shared a meal with a man for a very long time, and the thought of it made her shiver.

It's not a date, it's a good deed, she told herself.

But then she shouldn't feel this anticipation.

She heard the trunk door slam shut, and in a

second Connor was beside her, handing her the keys. "Thanks again for so much . . . efficiency. I'll be ready at five."

Once out of sight of the hotel, Leslie checked the car clock and noticed it was already three. She hadn't even checked in with the office all day, something she usually did every few hours. She and Gillian shared a small suite and secretary with a graphic artist and free-lance writer in a suburban office park. It was an extraordinarily convenient arrangement in which they could split overhead costs and use each other's services "as needed."

Leslie stopped at a service station pay phone and checked with the secretary for messages. There was nothing urgent, nothing that would give her an excuse to cancel dinner. So she headed for a nearby grocery store.

Potluck. If Connor MacLaren took potluck from what was in her refrigerator at the moment, he would be disappointed indeed. If she remembered correctly, there were two containers of yogurt, a half quart of milk—unless Robin had been into it—and some salad makings.

What would a Scotsman like?

Leslie's stomach seemed to tighten as she realized how important tonight had become. It had been a very long time since she'd been this attracted to a man. After the two years of unmitigated hell with Tommy, Leslie had believed herself immune to men and romance, especially at the grand old age of thirty-seven, soon to be thirty-eight. She was happy with her life, with her daughter, and with her career. She didn't need or want any more. Certainly not a man, and especially not another musician. So why was she so worried about what to feed him?

"Damn," she whispered, noting that she had never said so many damns in one day before. Not even in a year. This was all nonsense. Fretting over one meal was nonsense. She was suddenly fantasizing in a way she'd never done before, and she didn't understand it.

It was the kilt. It was simply that he was so different from all the other men she met: The soft brogue and the lilting sound of his words, the alluring magic of his voice and guitar. It was that, and nothing else.

That matter decided, she made her way to the grocery store, still uncertain what to buy.

She wondered again, what did a Scotsman like to eat?

And then, unbidden, came the other thought that had been pricking at her since she first saw him come through the gate at the airport.

What does a Scot wear under his kilt?

Three

Connor MacLaren *was* tired.

He had two hours to rest, no more, but he looked forward to seeing Leslie Turner again. He didn't know why, but he felt good just being with her, and that hadn't happened to him for a very long time.

Not since Annie.

He walked over to the ceiling-to-floor windows in his hotel room and looked down, knowing he should try to grab some sleep but too keyed up to do so.

His thoughts kept turning to Leslie. She puzzled him in many ways. She had been reserved in the beginning, even hostile, but as the day had worn on, a natural warmth emerged, one that made him feel comfortable and content.

Annie had had that kind of personality. Annie, who had died eight years ago with their ten-year-old son. Annie Laurie, he had called her, and he had always started a concert with that song—until that day in California when the telephone call came. He had not played the song since, even when it was requested, which it often was. He didn't think he could ever play that song again.

He had asked women out in recent years, of course. He was no monk and had no particular desire to be one. He liked women, and he was human, but he avoided anything that rang of permanence. He liked what he did, singing and traveling, and that didn't go with having a family. He had lived with guilt for years, because he wasn't in Edinburgh when his wife and son were killed in an accident. His wife, he had been told, lost control of the car in a rainstorm. If he had been home, if he had been driving, the two people he loved most of all would still be alive.

He knew he couldn't go through anything like that again—that if he remarried, he would have to curtail his traveling. And that would mean he'd have to give up what he did best and how he made his living. He could not survive solely on concerts in Edinburgh and other Scottish cities. He needed the exposure from worldwide concerts and appearances to sell his recordings.

But sometimes he became lonely, especially when he remembered how it had felt on returning home to Annie and Douglas. The quiet joy, the sense of belonging. Now he went home to an empty cottage with ghosts as furniture, and consequently he had contracted this year for a longer tour.

Leslie had brought back memories of his wife. They both had auburn hair, although Annie's had been more red. Annie had blue eyes and Leslie's were green, but they had the same fire in them, and there was a quiet, determined constancy he recognized, a constancy that scared him now just as it had years ago when he'd met Annie.

And so part of him quaked when he thought of this evening. Leslie had said her daughter was seventeen. A year younger than Doug would have been. She didn't look as if she could have a child that old.

Fool. He called himself that and a few other less than complimentary terms. He was only going to dinner, to "potluck," and he would be in Atlanta just a few days. Leslie was being kind to a client, nothing more. He was simply imagining the attraction between them. He had been tired, and perhaps a bit lonely on the beginning stretch of four months of hotel rooms.

Nonetheless, he found himself calling the hotel florist and ordering a bouquet of roses. He then found the flask in his luggage and poured himself a dram of scotch.

Connor went again to the wall of windows. A haze had settled over the city, but he could still see the islands of green. It reminded him a little of Edinburgh.

He decided he liked Atlanta.

Leslie saw the roses as she arrived at the hotel to pick up her guest. The bouquet was large and lovely, and came as a distinct shock. It had been a very long time since anyone had brought her roses. Since never, in fact.

Her eyes then fell on the man who held the flowers. Connor MacLaren was no longer wearing a kilt, but was dressed casually in a pair of tan cotton trousers and a light blue linen shirt with the sleeves rolled up. The color of his shirt made his eyes appear even bluer, like the deeper part of the sea.

If he was tired at all, he didn't show it. His stride, as he moved toward the car—the roses in one hand, the guitar in the other as requested—showed the same energy she'd seen earlier in the day.

Despite his full hands, Connor opened the car door and gave the roses to her. "Thank you, they're lovely," she said.

"And not nearly enough thanks for your dinner."

"Don't you think you'd best wait and see?"

"I have the second sight," he admitted modestly as he stored his guitar in the backseat and arranged his long physique in the seat next to her.

He was freshly shaven, and his hair was still a little damp from the shower. She felt a strong urge to run her fingers through the slightly curling strands. He smelled like soap and something else utterly enticing.

Needing a safe subject to talk about, she asked, "Did you get any rest?"

"An hour or so, but I don't need much when I'm traveling."

"I heard you tell Jan you enjoy touring. Don't you ever get tired of it?"

"Nay. Not yet. Perhaps someday, but not now. Many of the places I'll go, I've been before, and there are friends tae see." He shrugged, but it wasn't careless, more of a boyishly exuberant gesture. "And then there's the new places, new sights tae see and people tae meet." They were at a red light, and she turned to look at him. His eyes were intense as he said the last words, giving them a certain importance, making sure she understood that she was not the least of those people.

"And you like that?"

"Very much. Wouldn't you?"

She shook her head. "I don't think so. I like a home, a place to belong."

She saw a muscle tick in his cheek, and then someone behind them honked his horn. The light had changed. This displacement of attention was becoming a very disconcerting habit.

"You have a bonny city," he said, breaking the growing tension in the car.

"It is, isn't it?" she replied quickly, and started

to point out landmarks. "I live about fifteen minutes away when there's no traffic, but here . . ." Her voice trailed off apologetically as she stopped in the midst of a traffic cluster.

Connor merely sank more in his seat, looking totally at ease. "It's the way of cities."

"And Edinburgh?"

"Edinburgh, tae, with its narrow wee streets. But it's a lovely city, filled with history and ghosts."

"That you sing about . . ."

"Aye, I love each of them, those glorious ghosts of the past."

Leslie felt herself tingle inside as she heard his enthusiasm. She had never met anyone so full of life, so completely compelling, so . . . overwhelming.

"And you, Leslie, do you enjoy your job, shepherding souls through your city?"

Leslie hesitated. "That's Gillian's forte."

"And what do *you* usually do?"

"Plan promotions, brochures, develop advertising, mainly for real estate developments." It suddenly sounded very dull to her, although she loved her business, loved creating images, relished being an active part of Atlanta's growth. But next to his "ghosts," it was tame indeed.

"From what I've heard of Atlanta," he said slowly, "I would think that very fascinating."

Leslie's heart thumped a little faster. He seemed truly interested, which, for some reason, she hadn't expected.

"It is," she said. "I've watched Atlanta grow in so many ways, and it feels good to be a part of it."

"And . . . Gillian? How did you tae get together?"

Leslie laughed. "Sometimes we both wonder. She loves music and nightlife and excitement, and I like nice solid things. She's like a summer storm, and I'm like, well . . . " She searched for a word that wouldn't sound too boring.

"Like a summer's dawn," he said, his voice low and thoughtful.

She just barely managed to keep her gaze on the road. What a lovely image! Did he, could he really, believe that? An ache, a deep, yearning need, floated into her heart and seemed to lodge like a stone there. She felt her hands tighten around the steering wheel.

She wanted to ask how she was like a summer's dawn, but that would be fishing. Moreover, she wasn't sure she wanted to hear the answer. She couldn't allow herself to care about Connor Mac-Laren, a touring musician who would be here one week and then gone forever.

Connor watched her face, the first flush of pleasure and then confusion. Summer's dawn. The comparison had come so quickly. Fresh and tranquil and lovely. She was like that when she lowered her guard and gave a smile that was breathtaking. There was also constancy, a core of iron beneath that gentle surface.

He wondered about the flashes of hostility. He had no doubt they were rare and that she had to work at it.

"Musicians," he said suddenly, recalling the earlier conversation. "You ha' certain . . . reservations?"

The question took Leslie by surprise. She had almost forgotten her earlier lapse of manners. She winced as she recalled her previous behavior.

"My husband was a musician."

"I take it he isn't exactly a recommendation for others."

"No." The answer rang of bitterness. "And it's past tense. He's dead."

Silence followed, and Leslie was glad Connor

didn't say he was sorry, but instead merely looked as if he was digesting the information.

She thought she should resent his question, but she didn't. He apparently always spoke his mind, and refused to accept less from anyone else. And, in a way, she felt relieved. Just saying the words had lessened the pressure, the memories, that had started building inside.

"I think we decided," he said finally, "that all Americans and all Scots are not alike. Can you believe it's also true of musicians?"

The teasing challenge in his voice awakened her competitive nature. "I'll try," she said.

She heard his deep, throaty chuckle, and it made all her senses hum. "Such reluctance," he observed. "I see I have my work cut out for me."

Leslie risked a look in his direction.

"Tae change your mind," he added with a grin.

Part of her knew he already had. For Pete's sake, wasn't she taking him home for dinner, something she'd never done before with a client? She tried to tell herself she was doing it as a simple courtesy to a stranger to the city. But she knew, as well as she knew anything, that Connor MacLaren would never be a stranger long, wherever he went. If he crash-landed on Mars, he would immediately charm the martians into doing his every bidding.

He must have read her thoughts, as he had seemed to do ever since they met.

"And you are especially kind tae ask me tae dinner," he said, sounding more Scottish than ever, mischief dancing in each word. "A lonely Scot in a strange city."

"I don't think you're ever in a strange place," she said, and she meant it as a compliment. "Or lonely."

"Not entirely true," he said, with an odd, serious note in his voice. "But I try not tae let myself be."

"Does it work that way?" Never having been able

to control that part of life, those bleak moments of loneliness, she was curious.

"Not always," he said honestly. At his disarmingly frank reply she felt a strong empathy.

"Tell me about your daughter?" The question was wistful, and once more a part of her, a piece of her soul, reached out toward him. She recalled her question about his family, and his answer: *There is no one now.*

Had there been once? Was he widowed? Divorced?

"She's a senior in high school, and off to college next year."

"And is she a musician tae?"

"No, thank God," she said, before remembering her passenger's occupation. But he only chuckled again good-naturedly. "She's tone deaf like me."

"But she likes heavy metal?"

"Only because her friends do, I think," Leslie said. "I hope."

"And she's your only child?"

"Yes," Leslie answered without elaboration. She had wanted more—had, in fact, wanted a houseful. But it hadn't happened.

Connor was silent, and she glanced toward him. He was looking straight ahead now, not at her, and she saw the stiffness in his body. Again she wondered at the occasional glimpses of pain he revealed. But she herself was too much a private person to intrude on someone else's privacy.

"Tell me more about Scotland," she said instead, and she heard a sigh. Of relief? Of gratitude? She wished she didn't want to know so much, didn't care so much.

"It's a lovely green place," he began, "full of craggy mountains and bonny valleys, rugged shores and picturesque villages. You've never been there?"

She almost said nay, so infectious was his

accent, but she caught herself and shook her head. "I've never traveled outside the United States."

"And in the States?"

"A little . . . when my husband was on tour." She remembered that last tour. She had returned to the hotel room and found Tommy in bed with someone else. She had wanted to take the next plane home, but she had no money, and Tommy wouldn't give her any. Humiliated, she had finally called her parents.

As if Connor had sensed her pain, just as she had sensed his earlier, he turned the subject away from her. He asked where they were, and the location of the Scottish Festival.

"A few miles," she answered.

"Have you ever been?"

She shook her head. "I suppose it's like living in New York and never visiting the Empire State Building. You keep thinking you'll do it next time."

"And now you're trapped."

"Aye," she said with gentle mockery.

"I looked at the schedule. You surely don't mean tae accompany me through the entire week?"

"Part of our service," Leslie replied lightly.

"As well as dinner?"

"Only for lonely Scotsmen."

"I'm going tae have tae look like a waif more often."

Leslie had to smile at that. If anyone ever looked less like a waif . . .

They arrived at her house, a small, comfortable bungalow in one of the many older communities that surrounded Atlanta. It was near Stone Mountain Park, a very large state-owned park where the Scottish Festival would be held, and was in an excellent school district. The location had been ideal, and the house was within Leslie's budget.

She looked at it critically now, the old brick and the sprawling screen porch filled with comfortable but plain lawn furniture. The inside was similar— the furniture leaning toward comfortably stuffed rather than sleek, a hook rug on polished floors rather than plush carpet, the walls decorated with her daughter's good but amateur paintings.

Why did she ever invite him here?

But those piercing eyes looked around with approval rather than disappointment, and after they'd gone inside, he walked over to an easel where a canvas rested and tipped his head as he studied the painting.

"My daughter's," Leslie explained. "Her current enthusiasm."

"She's good. There's a lot of vitality in the lines."

Leslie studied him closely. His gaze was filled with interest, and after evaluating the painting, he went to the bookshelves. She had the strangest feeling that he was reading her rather than the titles.

"Robin should be home soon. She had a painting class after school. Would you like a drink while I start dinner?"

"If I can help you," Connor said, looking back at her, the reply more of an order than a question.

She wasn't at all sure she wanted his help. Her kitchen was small, and he already dominated this larger room.

Leslie was saved by the slamming of a door and the whirlwind that was Robin. Her daughter was in her artist phase and, like Gillian, looked like a Gypsy, her long brown hair starting to straggle from a ponytail on the right side of her head. She wore a wild T-shirt she had painted with a mishmash of colors and a pair of worn jeans she refused to give up.

"Mommmmmmm," she yelled, then gasped with surprise when she nearly ran into Connor Mac-Laren.

"Who are *you*?" she asked with something like awe.

"A bit of charity, I think."

"I've never seen a charity like you," Robin quipped, "or I would have volunteered long ago."

Connor chuckled. The girl was like a fresh breeze. He was enchanted as she grinned at him.

"Robin!" Leslie was partly amused, partly admonishing, and her tone held the I-think-I-should-say - something - though - I - don't - really - want - to undercurrent that she knew Robin recognized.

So did Connor MacLaren, if the twinkle in his eye meant anything.

"But you never brought anything like him home before," Robin explained in half-apology. Connor's chuckle turned into laughter while Leslie knew she was turning a bright shade of red.

"Robin," she said with more authority, "don't you need to change clothes?"

"Nope," Robin said happily as she glanced down at the new splotches of paint on her shirt. "You don't mind, do you, Mr. . . . ?"

"MacLaren," he supplied, his face softening in a way Leslie hadn't seen before.

"MacLaren." Her daughter tested the word. "I don't think I've heard your name before. But I like it," she quickly amended.

"Your mother inherited me," Connor explained seriously.

Robin regarded him very, very carefully. And then a light dawned in her face. "Ah . . . Aunt Gillian, no doubt. You look like an Aunt Gillian person."

Connor was obviously intrigued. "What's an Aunt Gillian person?"

"Sort of . . . untamed."

Connor considered that for a moment and raised an eyebrow. "Untamed?"

Robin eyed him speculatively, then nodded. "Yep."

"And what's one of your mother's persons?"

"Stuffy," Robin said quickly. "For instance—"

"Robin!" This time there was no question about her outrage.

Once more Connor roared with laughter, and even Leslie, though horrified by her daughter's unbridled comments, had to smile. Robin had always been precocious and blunt, older than her years in many ways because she'd had to be, with no father and Leslie working and gone so much. But Robin was nevertheless incurably whimsical. She was the light of Leslie's life, and Leslie nightly blessed her good fortune that Robin was Robin. Her worries had been minor ones.

"I think I'm glad I'm an Aunt Gillian person then," Connor finally managed.

"I love the way you talk," Robin said. "Will you teach me?"

Leslie rolled her eyes. "I think manners are the thing that need to be taught."

"I donna know if it could be taught."

"Do you think I could bottle it?" said the irrepressible Robin hopefully.

"And what kind of price would you put on it?"

"A high one," she shot back.

"Don't encourage her," Leslie broke in. "She's an entrepreneur as well as an artist."

"I'll watch myself," he said, "so I willna leave without a voice."

Robin gave him a look of approval, and then winked at her mother.

"Since you approve so much," Leslie said, "you can make the salad."

Robin looked at Connor and then at her mother. "Agreed," she said. "You stay here and entertain Mr.—"

"Connor," he said. "Please call me Connor."

"Hmmmm, I like that. Mom, why don't you make . . . Connor a drink?" She flew into the kitchen before Leslie had a chance to close her now-wide-open mouth.

"She's quite—"

Leslie's mouth closed. "I told you she was going on thirty."

"She's really quite wonderful. Is she always like that?"

"Most of the time. It's hard to keep up."

"You're very lucky, you know." He was serious, and she again sensed that sadness that seemed to haunt him. She wanted to wipe it away, and watch his eyes crinkle with humor instead.

"What would you like?" she said. "I have scotch, gin, and wine."

"Scotch," he replied. "Without ice."

"I'll be back in a minute."

Her knees almost buckled under her as she walked. In such a short time he had ambushed her usually composed feelings. Everything had been touched, every part of her, and it scared her.

"He's . . . too much, Mom. Who is he?"

She was assaulted by the question the second she entered the kitchen.

"He's a client," she answered, heading toward the bottles she'd set out before picking up Connor.

"But *who* is he? He's gorgeous."

"He's a singer, a folksinger. Not your type at all," Leslie said as her hands shook and spilled a little scotch on the table.

Get a hold of yourself, Leslie, she told herself. The rice was done; it only needed heating. She put that on a burner and took the marinated steaks out of the refrigerator. There was French bread, too, already sliced and buttered.

Robin stared as Leslie put the steaks in the oven. "Pretty fancy, Mom."

"He's a client," Leslie excused herself.

"Only a client? You've never brought one home before."

"Then how do you know they're stuffy?"

"I met Mr. Morrow at that restaurant. And I listen to you and Aunt Gillian. Developers and lawyers. Yuck."

Leslie shook her head. "Take the drink in."

"What about me?"

"A Coke will do you nicely."

Robin shrugged philosophically. "Ah well, he's intoxicating enough."

"Robin!"

"You're saying that a lot tonight," Robin commented, making her getaway, Connor's scotch in hand.

Leslie sighed as she gathered the salad ingredients. Well, perhaps it was just as well that Robin entertain their guest or they would never have dinner. Thank heaven she had already set the table.

She started slicing the cucumbers, each stroke growing a little stronger. She was not going to let him get to her. She wasn't. She wasn't.

She wasn't.

She heard laughter from the other room, and something inside her heart crunched. They sounded so good together, her daughter and the Scotsman. Robin took to people easily, she always had, but Leslie had never see her quite this . . . eager. She knew Robin missed having a father; she had mentioned it frequently as a child, although not in recent years. And now the girlish giggle and masculine laugh were uncommonly painful to Leslie. She damned Tommy once more. She couldn't let it happen again. Never.

Slice. She wasn't going to let Connor MacLaren get to her!

She wasn't!

Four

Connor looked at Leslie across the table and saw those green eyes sparkle as she regarded her daughter. Robin had put candles on the table at the last moment, and the flames' glow flickered across her mother's fine skin, adding a touch of mystery to her delicate features.

He was seeing another side of her. A hint of her earlier reserve remained, but even then she seemed to smile more readily, an open, lovely smile that warmed him to his toes.

He wondered about the husband who had apparently crippled the natural spirit that he suspected was once as free and ebullient as her daughter's. He felt a terrible anger at the man who'd made Leslie build a cocoon around herself, who'd made her so cautious with other men.

His gaze met hers, and he felt that sharp stab of physical awareness, the attraction that flashed between them so readily. She flushed and turned back to Robin.

Connor hadn't felt so alive in years.

The food was good without fuss, the meat cooked to perfection. He was reminded of another table, of Annie and Douglas, of quiet conversation and happy laughter. He wondered, with a terrible sense of guilt, if he had ever felt this electricity between himself and Annie. A quiet happiness, yes. Contentment, surely. But this challenge, this magnetism?

"Mom says you're going to be here all week," Robin said. "If you'll come to dinner again, I'll make my specialty."

"Should I ask what that might be?"

"No," Leslie answered. "I don't think you really want to know."

"Now, I'm intrigued."

"Then come," Robin begged.

Leslie interceded. "I think Mr. MacLaren is committed for the week."

Connor saw some of Robin's eagerness fade, and he was surprised at how much it touched him. Yet Leslie had just effectively asked him not to accept her daughter's invitation. "I have an alternate suggestion," he said. "Why don't you both accompany me tae the Tartan Ball Saturday night?"

"A ball?" Robin asked with the first reluctance he had seen in her.

"It's not that intimidating. If it's like the others I've attended, it'll be full of color and music and Scottish dancing. I'll even teach you a Highland dance or tae."

Robin's eyes brightened like lights on a Christmas tree, and she turned to Leslie. "Can we, Mom?"

Leslie hesitated, looking at Connor for a moment as if seeking some kind of answer to a question, and then back to Robin. She nodded.

"Mom told me you brought a guitar. You will sing for us, won't you?"

Connor couldn't resist a friendly goading. "Your mother said you liked another kind of music."

"She tells me I should broaden my tastes," Robin replied.

"Then I would be quite honored," he said in the same pseudoserious tone that Robin had affected.

She grinned at him as if they shared a secret, and Connor's heart ached as he thought of Douglas. He wondered what his son would have made of the impish delight across the table from him, and the desolation that had been so deep within him for years was suddenly blinding.

He missed a comment and realized it only when he noticed the piercing look Leslie directed at him. He was aware then of silence, the kind of pause that followed an unacknowledged question.

"Robin, why don't you get the dessert?" Leslie's voice echoed with understanding, and some of the pain seeped from him.

After Robin had left the table, Connor said. "I missed a question?"

"You missed a question," she confirmed. "You were a long way off."

"I'm sorry."

"Don't ever be sorry for feelings. It took me a long time to learn that."

"It's just that your daughter reminded me of . . ." He couldn't say the words "my son." He hadn't talked about Douglas and Annie to anyone, not even his brother.

"You mean there's more than one Robin running around in the world?"

Connor found one side of his mouth crooking up. "No, I think she must be unique."

Robin returned, and the dessert was consumed in companionable silence. Leslie had purchased a cheesecake from her favorite bakery, and she'd set up the automatic coffee maker earlier, plugging it in just before dinner.

Connor groaned as he finished. "I'm not sure I can get the guitar on my lap."

But within minutes he did, as they sat in the small living room lined with books. As always, the music took over all of Connor's emotions. He loved the songs, each with its own flavor. Some, like the "Skye Boat Song" and "Johnny, I Hardly Knew Ye," reflected both tragedy and longing, while the lilting "Gypsy Rover" was full of fun and whimsy. His music was his way of expelling his own grief, an excuse to exercise a sometimes irreverent humor. It carried him across seas and back centuries in time.

He concluded with the wistful, haunting "These Are My Mountains."

He'd seldom had a more transfixed audience. For a heavy-metal fan, Robin was sitting there with her mouth in an *O*, and Leslie's eyes were slightly glazed as if with mist. He had the sudden urge to lay down the guitar and take her in his arms. He wondered how those soft lips would feel, how her curved body would fit into his.

"Will you sing 'Annie Laurie'?" she asked, interrupting his thoughts.

The words penetrated like a sword, and he stiffened. "I'm sorry," he said more abruptly than he intended. "I don't sing that."

He put the guitar aside. "I think it's time tae go. You've been more than kind, and I've taken your complete day."

Connor saw the confusion, even hurt, flicker across her face at his curtness, but there had been too many memories tonight. The evening had made him long again for something he knew was impossible.

But she merely nodded.

"I'll clean up," Robin volunteered, obviously puzzled by the sudden tension. "And you've converted me, Connor. You beat heavy metal any day." She winked at him and disappeared out of the room.

Connor wanted to say something, but he couldn't. The mention of "Annie Laurie" had been too painful. He merely followed Leslie as she picked up her purse and started for the door.

He ducked his head in the kitchen. "It's been a pleasure, Robin."

"You bet. I'll be ready for the Tartan Ball."

"I might have a surprise," he said. "But don't tell your mother."

"Hmmmm . . . she needs a surprise."

He nodded, feeling suddenly better as an idea started to form in his mind. "Good night."

"I still want to bottle it," she replied.

Connor remained uncharacteristically quiet on the drive back to the hotel. He should have taken a cab, he decided, but his mind had been elsewhere when he'd followed Leslie to the car.

He shouldn't feel this way, soft and tender. He hadn't felt this way since Annie died. He thought he'd come to terms with the past, but now it was so damned real again, so fresh and painful.

Robin was part of it. She reminded him of Douglas, of his son's endless curiosity, of his excitement at Connor's homecomings, of the endless pleading to go on tour with him. But there had been school, and the road was no place for a child. Now, he wished he'd said to hell with school.

But even while Leslie and Robin brought back memories, he also realized they had reignited something in him, an inner fire that had been missing for so long. He didn't want to let them go, even though he knew how damaging any additional contact would be.

You don't have a choice now, he told himself. You've committed yourself to the ball, and Leslie's your guide for the next few days. The thought was both exhilarating and alarming, and he'd never felt that contradiction before.

He was startled when the car came to a stop in front of his hotel. He looked at Leslie, and there was an anxious, rather perplexed expression on her face. In the light of the hotel entrance their gazes met and held.

Connor knew better, but he couldn't stop himself. He leaned over, and his hand brushed the side of her face. Her skin was almost velvety, and incredibly tempting.

She didn't move, didn't try to avoid the caress, and his fingers ran down to her lips, stroking in a soft, questioning way, asking a silent question. He felt her tremble under his touch, and it made his own body tense with need, with awareness.

He moved closer, his lips pressing against hers with breezelike lightness. Another question.

Connor felt her respond, her lips meeting his with a desire of their own. Her breath was sweet and warm, her eyes wide and bright, a flame flickering deep within, and the tension in him started to prickle, each nerve ending responding to the touch and spreading messages that transformed his body into a sizzling firecracker, ready to explode. But he sensed the slightest hesitancy in Leslie, just enough to make him tender and restrained, even as his own needs wanted more, demanded more.

His lips wandered across hers, stroking, moving upward across her cheek and back again until her mouth opened. The kiss deepened, and their tongues hungrily explored each other, yearning spurring the tension between them. Electricity hummed, and then it exploded.

Her hands went up to his neck, her fingers caressing his skin, leaving little trails of fire. All his senses, all his reservations, were lost in the intensity of the contact. Longing so strong it rendered him all but senseless tore through him until he ached inside.

His hand went to her hair. It was incredibly silky in his fingers, spilling over in small, curling tendrils that teased his skin. Everything about her was soft. Soft and giving and fine . . .

The horn of a car sounded then, and he realized where they were. Reluctantly he moved away and watched the dazed expression in her face with wonder.

"Thank you," he whispered. "Thank you for a very fine day."

He watched as she swallowed and her self-composure returned, the remarkable composure that guarded so much fire.

She straightened, a hand going to her hair to flick a curl from her forehead. She bit her lip, an endearing, uncertain gesture that captured a piece of his heart.

"Tomorrow," she finally said, obviously struggling to sound matter-of-fact. "Eight-thirty."

"Eight-thirty," he confirmed.

He started to leave the car, then turned back. "You're a lovely lady, Leslie Turner. And you have a lovely daughter."

Her eyes closed for a moment, and then opened. "Good night, Connor," she said with finality, and started the car.

He had no choice but to shut the door. He took his guitar case from the back seat and stood on the curb as she drove off, a little faster than before. He watched until the taillights of the car disappeared.

Leslie never knew how she made it home that night without running off the road. She hadn't felt so confused and out of control for years. She'd never responded to a man like this before.

It was as if she had turned into someone else, had entered a place that was unreal and magical. Life wasn't like this. She was too old to believe in love at first sight. She was too experienced to succumb to charm.

But she'd been like putty moments earlier. Part of her rejoiced in those exhilarating feelings, and another part scoffed. Middle-aged fantasies.

You're not so old. Just thirty-seven.

Too old for this nonsense.

But her body still tingled from his touch, and her lips still trembled from the kiss, and his presence was still very much alive in the car. And she kept hearing the longing in his voice as he'd sung earlier.

It had been the tenderness that nearly struck her deaf and blind, his tenderness with her and the gentle teasing with her daughter. She'd never experienced either before, and she didn't know how to handle it.

He's an entertainer, she reminded herself. He'll be off in just a few days. Keep it light—or the pain might be very heavy.

She tried keeping it light. She tried very hard the next day.

It hadn't helped that Robin had met her at the door last night, wanting to know every detail.

"He's awesome," she'd said with a sigh.

Such unmitigated praise didn't come often from her daughter. Robin knew her father had abandoned her mother even before she was born, and she didn't trust easily. Leslie had feared the knowledge had left a scar, for Robin dated rarely, and then mostly boys she considered "friends."

Robin had also been critical of the few men Leslie had gone out with over the years, and Leslie had wondered whether it had been jealousy or a hurt that Robin felt deeply but didn't express.

But last night, Robin had been filled with enthusiasm, and Leslie finally surmised that it was because Connor MacLaren presented no danger. Robin knew the singer was in Atlanta only a week.

So Leslie had done her best today to keep the atmosphere professional and distant. Her heart and senses had become too involved last night, and she didn't intend for it to happen again.

It was Tuesday. Gillian had arranged an interview on a morning talk show, then with the daily newspaper, and finally a radio program in the afternoon, which meant a hectic schedule. Connor charmed everyone he met, including a usually abrasive entertainment editor at the newspaper. Leslie left them alone, not wanting the reporter to feel she didn't trust her client, or that he needed any help. At a discreet distance she watched Connor weave his magic.

When he was finally finished, striding through the newsroom with that restless, confident gait of his, every woman's eyes on him, Leslie felt a twinge of pain inside her. It would always be like this with Connor MacLaren. He would always turn heads.

Leslie felt her stomach twist in a particularly nasty way.

Her voice was very cool as he reached her. "It looked as if it went well."

One of his eyebrows rose at the frost in her voice. "He's very knowledgeable," he said. "I liked him."

She couldn't help but raise an eyebrow of her own. Gillian had a number of stories about the reporter, none of them flattering. "You might be a majority of one then," she said.

He grinned. "He's been tae Scotland. We talked about pubs."

Leslie could only shake her head in an admiration she really didn't want to entertain.

"Where tae now?" he asked, that easy grin of his widening, like that of a little boy who had accomplished a difficult task and was now expecting approval.

She hesitated. It was lunchtime and she wasn't altogether sure she could survive another meal with Connor. Not when he wore that darn kilt. How could any man look so compellingly masculine in a skirt?

It was as if he'd read her mind. "Lunch?"

She nodded, trapped. He had a two o'clock appointment, and it was hardly worthwhile to take him back to the hotel, leave him there, and pick him up again. "What do you like?"

"Do you really want tae know?" he said, his eyes sparkling.

The implication was clear, and she felt shivers shoot down her back. It was the first time today he'd referred to last night, to anything personal at all, in fact. She'd had the impression he was trying to ignore the previous evening as much as she.

But now those brief moments were out in the open, and she felt the tension again, the fiery attraction radiating between them. Warmth curled in her stomach as their gazes locked, unwanted messages exchanged between two reluctant recipients. Suddenly she knew that he, with all his confidence, was experiencing the same fear she was.

"I wasn't going tae let this happen today," he said.

"Me either," she said with the smallest of wry smiles.

But still they didn't move from the hallway where they stood. In some corner of her mind Leslie thought that people must be passing by. but all she saw was the dark blue of his eyes, the intense brilliant blue that revealed a turmoil of his own, and that knowledge seeped into her soul and made him vulnerable and even more irresistible than before.

If that were in any way possible.

Someone bumped into her, apologizing briefly before hurrying on, and that broke the silence between them.

"We'd better hurry," she said breathlessly.

"Aye," he replied in a low voice. "Or I might be embarrassing the both of us."

Leslie decided not to explore that statement. "What about a local landmark?"

She saw the slightest suspicion on his face. He was right to have it.

Lunch was at the Varsity, the biggest, noisiest, least private restaurant in the nation. Connor in his attire hardly rated attention mixed in between men with business suits, Georgia Tech students in cutoff shorts, and construction workers in almost everything. A television blared in the room where they carried their trays, and they sat in schoollike desk seats.

"Are you trying tae tell me something, Ms. Turner?" he asked as he took a bite of a chili dog.

"Everyone comes to the Varsity," she said. "Even the vice president a few weeks ago."

"Is that a recommendation?"

"It all depends on the way you look at it," Leslie retorted, partly satisfied that they would not be alone in a romantic restaurant, partly frustrated by the same fact.

"May I choose the place tomorrow?"

She sighed. "We do have another day tomorrow, don't we?"

"Is that resignation?"

"I don't know what it is."

"Will you have dinner with me tonight?" He hadn't meant to say that. In fact, he had decided last night to keep his distance. But he couldn't, not when he was with her. He wanted to prolong each moment.

Leslie had decided to refuse if, by some miracle, he asked. "Yes," she said.

They didn't hear the noon news droning on. They didn't even hear the loud quarreling voices next to them.

"A place with candlelight," he said.

"Yes," she agreed.

"I'll pick you up."

"But . . ."

"I rented a car."

"You didn't tell me," she accused.

"I was afraid you'd turn me loose."

"You'll never find your way to my house."

"I have a terrrrrific incentive," he said huskily. "I like challenges."

She believed him. He had obviously made his way around cities all over the world. She could probably leave him the rest of Gillian's interview schedule and, as he said, turn him loose.

It was not a happy thought, she realized. Deserting him would not be professional, she rationalized.

Hiding behind that excuse, she tried to pay attention to the newscast until it was time to go. But she didn't hear a word. She could only think of dinner tonight. Alone. With Connor MacLaren.

She wondered about the hole she was digging for herself.

Five

He had been right. He did make it. Right on time.

Robin had even changed to a less gaudy T-shirt in anticipation of Connor's visit.

Leslie, who had just entered the living room, noticed that. And she wasn't sure she liked it.

She was still having second thoughts about this evening, had been ever since this afternoon when she had dropped Connor off at the hotel.

She had gone back to her office and checked messages. There was one from Gillian, the usual breezy recital of events, but when Leslie tried to return the call, Gillian was out. Leslie then returned a call to Steve Morrow, the developer who was currently their most important client. He was having a grand opening for a multimillion-dollar country-club development in three weeks, and needed reassurance that all their plans were set.

Once that was done, she checked with several other clients to make sure everyone was happy, and then she just stared at the door for an hour, wondering why her mind was wandering to the dinner tonight instead of staying on business.

The Word Shop, except for Robin, was the most important thing in her life. It represented

security and achievement, a process of growing.
After Tommy had left her, she had a baby and no
money. The tabloids had made her life pure mis-
ery with their constant reporting of Tommy's affairs, and that, plus Tommy's own cruel remarks,
had made her feel less than nothing. It had taken
years to restore her confidence, years of work and
sacrifice and overcoming so many demons. But the
Word Shop was now hers—hers and Gillian's—
and she usually enjoyed her work tremendously.

She didn't like the feeling now that maybe it
wasn't enough. It *had* been enough for years.

Why had she consented to dinner?

Because it was impossible to say no to Connor
MacLaren. She was absolutely sure of that. But
she had to learn; she was absolutely sure of that
too.

As he walked into her house, she knew why. She
couldn't say she didn't love the way he looked in
the kilt. But now . . .

He was no less than magnificent in a pair of
dark blue slacks, a blue-gray shirt, a wool blue-
and-gray tweed sports jacket, and a dark blue tie.

"Totally wow," Robin blurted out.

Connor gave her that disarming grin of his. "Is
that approval?"

"Sure," Robin said, "and I know something else
I want to bottle now."

His grin widened. "I wouldn't mind keeping a bit
of you around either."

"Only a bit?" Robin queried.

He winked. "You'll have tae tell me how much
goes in a bottle."

Robin eyed him. "Will you pose for me sometime? Mom says you look terrific in a kilt."

"Ah, she did, did she?" he asked with amusement as Connor saw Leslie's face suffuse with red.
"You can tell her she looks terrific in green."

Robin looked from one to the other. "I think you

should tell each other, and I have some homework to do. But will you pose for me?"

"He's not going to have time, Robin," Leslie cut in.

"But I'll make a wee bit of time," he said. "No one's ever wanted tae paint me before."

"Strange," Robin muttered as she dashed upstairs, ignoring Leslie's horrified expression. At the top of the stairs Robin paused. "When?"

Connor looked at Leslie. "Tomorrow afternoon? There's nothing on the schedule."

"But don't you have people you have to see? . . ." Her voice trailed off. Robin's expression was losing some of its brightness. "Of course it's all right," she amended.

Robin grinned. "Stay out as late as you want," she said in a motherly way, then disappeared down the hall before Leslie could say anything.

Leslie wasn't even aware of what she ate that night. She *was* aware of women looking at them, of the waiter's almost embarrassing solicitude after being given a taste of Connor's charm. She was aware of how blue Connor's eyes were, and how his mouth twisted when he smiled and how white his teeth were. Dear God, how aware she was. She kept thinking how wonderful his lips would feel against her skin again, and remembering how well his fingers twined with hers as he had seized her hand on the way in. Seized it and squeezed with a sudden intimacy that warmed her all the way through.

Their eyes often met, and Leslie found herself playing with her knife, eating a roll she didn't want, anything to distract herself from that direct gaze that seemed to reach straight inside to her most private self.

"Robin's very special," he said.

Nothing could have disarmed her more. "I think so," she replied.

"Is she always so spontaneous?"

Leslie nodded. It was true, except around men. Leslie was afraid that some of her own cautious feelings in that regard had rubbed off on her daughter.

"Does she have much school left?"

"She graduates in May."

"And then?"

"College . . . she'll probably study art."

He was silent for a few moments. "I expect you will miss her."

Though she lived with that fear, she merely shrugged. "Tremendously. But that's part of being a parent."

"But with just the tae of you . . . ?"

It was a prying statement, but said with such sympathy that Leslie found herself addressing something that had been lurking in the back of her mind for some time. She had made her daughter so much of her life, wanting to make up for Robin's not having a father, and now she often wondered about the loneliness inherent in that absorption.

Perhaps that was why she was presently so vulnerable.

Her eyes met Connor's, and she saw an emptiness of his own in them. Her hand reached across the table for his. His fist tensed, and she knew exactly how he felt. The air around them was pregnant with sensations reaching between them, expressing emotions that didn't need words.

It was the most spellbinding—and frightening—experience she'd ever had. Her blood had turned to hot lava, flowing on an inexorable course through her body.

"I don't usually do this," he said shakily. At her inquisitive look he added, "Go courting in a city."

Courting. The word had an old-world feel to it, just as so many other things about him did. *Courting.* It was a particularly endearing word. A word with promises. But there could be no promises. Leslie knew that. She didn't believe in promises.

She tried to make her comment light. "No girl in every city?"

"No. And you?"

Leslie heard an intensity in the question that surprised her. Though compelled to answer in the same direct way, she was still too confused to speak. She shook her head.

"And how could that be with such a bonny lass?" he asked with a lilt that told her he was trying to cut through the tension between them.

"I could ask you the same question, my troubadour," she finally said.

"My troubadour," he repeated, rolling the latter word around in his mouth, the final *r* echoing across the table that had been cleared and now held only half-filled wineglasses. "I like the way you say that."

"A modern-day troubadour, wandering from city to city, footloose and free. It must be a wonderful life." Leslie was trying her best to emphasize certain realities.

"Most of the time," he qualified. "It does, on occasion, get lonely."

"And in Edinburgh?"

He shrugged. "At times."

Leslie couldn't hold back the question any longer. "You're so good with Robin. You don't have children?" She remembered his negative reply when she had asked about his family.

Connor studied her for several minutes as if

weighing whether he should answer. "I had a son, Douglas. He and his mother were killed in a car accident. He was ten at the time. He would be just a little older than Robin now." There was an incredible wistfulness in his voice, a grief that was still fresh no matter how long ago the accident had been.

Leslie wished she hadn't asked. It had, after all, been none of her business. She suddenly wondered how she would feel if anything ever happened to Robin, but she couldn't even begin to imagine.

"I'm sorry," she whispered. "I shouldn't have . . ."

"There's nothing you shouldn't do," he interrupted. "There's something between us . . . I think we both know that. I don't know what, but I do know I want tae spend time with you. A great deal of time."

"And then you'll leave?"

"And then I'll leave," he answered gently. "But let's take what we can."

"I don't know if I can do that."

"Afraid?" It wasn't a challenge but a query.

"Yes."

He grinned. "Me tae."

"It's hard to believe that."

"But true."

Leslie wished she didn't believe him. She wished he didn't have that entrancing burr in his voice. She wished he didn't smile as he did, and that his eyes didn't crinkle with amusement, and that he didn't have that dry, droll sense of humor. She wished all that, and she wished more. She wished that it were twenty-two years ago . . . before Tommy, before the disillusionments, before the pain. Before the fear of being hurt again.

"Are you ready tae go, Leslie?" He had been

watching her closely, she knew, and she wondered what had just flickered in her face, how many thoughts she'd revealed.

She wasn't ready. She didn't want to leave, because then she would lose him. Now, it was only the two of them. There was no past, no future, only these minutes during which she savored an intimacy and closeness she'd never felt before.

"Home?"

"No. Not yet. Do you have a suggestion?"

A wild streak of joy ran through Leslie. "What about Stone Mountain Park? It's really pretty."

"Done."

Leslie knew there would be a price to pay for her recklessness, but at that moment she didn't care.

The park was active, just as it was nearly every hour of the day. During the mornings joggers filled the paths running alongside the roads. Later families packed the picnic grounds and various attractions, and at night teenagers "cruised" the roads.

Leslie felt like a teenager herself. She had instinctively moved toward Connor, and one of his hands was over hers. The night was beautiful, a full moon hanging in the sky surrounded by millions of twinkling pieces of light.

It was October, one of the nicest months in Atlanta, a time when the trees changed color and night brought the faintest bite of chill to preempt the warmth of the daytime sun.

Leslie directed Connor to where the games would be held and showed him the coliseum where the Tattoo was to take place in two nights. Then they left the car and walked along a lighted path.

"All the green reminds me of Edinburgh," he said. "You must visit me there someday. I would like showing it tae you."

The seemingly innocent statement punctured Leslie's balloon. This time, this sudden magic, was temporary, and she had to remember that.

It was as if he were reminding himself, too, for he impulsively swung her to him, and his lips pressed hard against hers with a kind of desperation.

The world seemed to erupt in a giant field of flame. If he hadn't been holding her close, she might have fallen, for her legs were nothing more than wax in the inferno and her heart no more than fuel. There was so much strength in his body, so much heat, so much harsh longing. She felt his lips search for a response, and then the kiss deepened as her mouth opened and welcomed him.

His lips were gentle but insistent. They seared her mouth with warmth and hunger as her hands crept up his back and played with the thick hair. One of his arms reached around her and pulled her tight against him, and she felt every hard curve of his body and relished every exploratory touch of his tongue. They inflamed her body, made her weak with a longing so strong, she thought she'd be consumed with it.

His mouth left her lips, wandering along her face, grazing her cheeks, caressing the area around her eyes, whispering in her ears, stroking her throat. Each touch was infinitely tender, searching rather than demanding, promising rather than taking.

The coolness of the evening was gone now, lost in a fever of need. She didn't care if this was a public park, that anyone might come along. She didn't care about anything except the wonderful, remarkable way Connor MacLaren made her feel. So alive. So electric. So wonderfully *feeling*.

The mother, the professional, the onlooker, were

all gone now. She felt all the needs she'd bottled up for so long exploding from pure fermentation, and Connor was the catalyst.

Their lips met again, his moving back to claim her mouth, and the night became dazzling, a kaleidoscope of brilliant colors and images and emotions. Leslie felt as if she'd just been born, fresh and untouched and . . . wanted.

Connor's tongue reached inside her mouth, stoking little blazes that flared like freshly lighted candles caught by the breeze, and she found herself responding with raw hunger. She felt the sensuous tickling of his lips against her face. Every part of her body was uniquely sensitive now.

His mouth tore away from hers. "Leslie," he said with a moan. "Lass . . . this . . . isn't the place. I want you tae much."

Want. The word set off warning bells in her head. That was all this was: Want. Physical need. No magic here, just good old-fashioned lust. What had she expected, anyway? Vows of undying love after two days? Nonetheless, her stomach plummeted.

Years ago, she'd allowed her emotions and hormones to rule her, and she'd walked into hell. She didn't regret that time, because it had produced Robin, but neither would she ever be a victim again, a thing, a toy.

She straightened, consciously moving away from him both physically and emotionally. It hurt, it took all her strength. But she did it, and she saw puzzlement flash across his face.

"I think we'd better go," she said, and even she heard the chill in her voice.

"All right," he replied quietly.

Leslie didn't speak on the short drive back to her house; neither did she sit as close to Connor as she had earlier. Fear had overtaken her, an icy-cold wave that sent desolation washing through her. She had made her compromises with life and had been satisfied with them. But in just a few days that had changed. She knew there was more now, so much more, and she was so greedy for it. But the more she tasted, the more she knew she would eventually hurt.

When they reached the house, Connor started to leave the car, but she stopped him with a hand. "No," she said. "It's late, and I'd better go inside."

He studied her cautiously, even a bit grimly. "Tomorrow then?"

"You don't need me now," she replied evenly. "You have a car . . . you can get around."

"But I promised Robin I would pose for her," he said with devilish humor, "and I don't have that many chances tae become immortal."

"You still don't," she said lightly. "I doubt whether Robin's phase will make a lasting impression in the art world."

"It will make a lasting impression on me," he replied, serious again, all the humor gone, and Leslie heard what she didn't want to hear: A poignant loneliness.

For the life of her she couldn't deny it. Nor could she disappoint Robin. At least, that's what she told herself. "At five, then," she said.

"And I'll lose you . . . as a guide during the day?"

"You need me like you need an extra head."

"But will you come with me tomorrow? You know these reporters."

"And you'll probably know them better in ten minutes than I have in years." It was a galling admission. But correct if what she'd seen in the past two days held true. Despite her job, she had kept the press at a distance, acting like a professional but making no attempt to befriend individual reporters. She had too many bad memories of the tabloids from years ago. It had, in fact, taken mammoth willpower in the beginning to deal even with the more responsible members of the media. But she had done it, and now it came easier; nevertheless, she maintained a certain protective wall.

"You've done a great job, you know," he said. "My agent in New York has already received calls about bookings because of the television appearance yesterday. And you *do* help, just being there." He reached over and clasped her hand. "Thank you."

He'd done it again, defused all her fears, all her reservations, with just a few words and a thank you that sounded utterly sincere. She was practically consumed with a need to reach over and touch him again, to run her hand through his hair.

Go, she told herself. Go while you can. And she did, getting out of the car, hesitating only a moment before shutting the door, and doing so only when she saw him start to follow.

She then ran up the stairs, her key in her hand. She quickly went inside . . . without looking back. Leaning against the door, she felt like the biggest coward in all of Atlanta.

If not the world.

Connor spent much of the night sleepless. All the male parts of him were complaining. The king-size bed was lonely. The offerings on the television were far from adequate in taking his mind away from Leslie. She had become implanted firmly in his heart; every time he tried to direct his thoughts away from her, he kept seeing that appealingly uncertain smile.

In the beginning he had been attracted because of the physical resemblance to Annie—or so he thought. But now he'd discovered the women weren't alike at all, that he cared for Leslie Turner for herself, for her bright intelligence, her quick sense of humor, her loving relationship with her daughter. He admired her independence and the strength that had developed a successful business. It stimulated him, challenged him.

Annie, on the other hand, had been very happy to stay at home. She had been shy and did not enjoy traveling with him, preferring their small cozy house and her books. They had known each other nearly all their lives, having grown up together on a small Edinburgh street, and he had protected her through their childhood years. They had always been friends, and they had drifted into marriage. He had loved her in an undemanding way, had loved her sweetness, but she'd never aroused a fever in his blood like the one he'd felt tonight.

That didn't mean, though, that he missed her any less, missed her quiet presence that had made such a comfortable, loving home for him and his son, nor did it lessen the guilt he still felt. He should never have left her alone so much.

Which brought him back to all the reasons he should stop seeing Leslie Turner except on a purely professional basis. There was no future with her, and he didn't want to hurt her. Dammit, he didn't want to hurt himself. But they were like spontaneous combustion together. He'd never experienced anything like the explosive nature of being near her, and he didn't know how to handle it.

When he finally gave up on sleep in the early morning hours, he took a cold shower, which, he thought, he should have done the night before to lessen the tension in his body. He slowly dressed, donning his kilt, shirt, and leather vest.

Then the phone rang, and he knew before answering it who it was.

He couldn't stop the waves of pleasure that rolled through him when he heard her soft Southern voice.

He didn't even want to.

Six

Dressed in his kilt and jacket, his guitar in his hand, Connor MacLaren was standing just outside the hotel waiting for Leslie when she arrived at the hotel.

Her heartbeat accelerated when he smiled in a particular way she hadn't seen before. It was private and intimate, and obviously just for her. Any recriminations she had about her own behavior fled as she found herself responding to him with a delighted smile of her own.

She was suddenly very glad she had called him, even though she'd done so only after a night of painful soul-searching.

Leslie had always urged her daughter to take chances with her life, to go after what she wanted. She had supported Robin when she took up dance, and then piano, and finally painting. Try, she had told her daughter. Explore your world and discover what is best for you.

Had she been the world's biggest hypocrite? You don't achieve anything if you don't try, she had counseled Robin. You may not get hurt, but then you don't have the great joys either.

She'd felt such joy last night. The dinner had

been wonderful, the aftermath glorious. She'd felt giddy and marvelous and young. She'd experienced the rush of blood for the first time in many years, and in Connor's tenderness had known a sensation of being wanted she'd *never* had.

Had Tommy crippled her that badly?

And was she really going to let him, even now, continue to have that kind of impact on her life?

When she'd found her own private answer, she'd called Connor to say she would like to accompany him today. Any doubt she still harbored disappeared as he stepped into her car, his presence nearly overpowering.

"A bonny morning," he said, the burr vibrating through her senses like a glass of aged, warmed brandy. "And you look beautiful."

No one could look quite as good as he did. No one should, darn it. But little lines ringed his eyes, and she suspected that he, like her, had won precious little sleep last night. Still, just gazing at him lifted her feeling of leaden weariness.

She remembered last night, and every one of her senses came electrically alive. She longed to reach over to touch him, to feel his lips against her skin. . . . Just the thought sent shivers down her back.

"I would dearly gi' a half pound tae know what you're thinking," he said, and Leslie wondered if everything she'd thought had been reflected in her face. Dear God, she hoped not. Where was the famous control Gillian always said she admired?

Gone to hell in a hand basket, Leslie answered herself.

"You keep me off balance," she said, starting the car and driving off.

"Ah, do I, lass? And just as well, because you do the same tae me."

That was difficult to believe. She'd never met anyone who seemed so on balance, so accepting of the world and everything in it. Except for those fleeting moments of pain when he mentioned his family. The thought caused an empathic ache in her heart.

"It's hard to think of you off balance."

"Believe me, it happens, particularly in the past forty-eight hours."

Leslie glanced at him and caught the bafflement in his face as he completed the sentence, but then the grin that followed dazzled her again.

He'd even dazzled Robin, who was usually hard to impress. She remembered their conversation this morning.

Her daughter had viewed her with interest. "You look really pretty, Mom," she said. "He's still coming over this afternoon, isn't he?"

"You like him, don't you, Robin?" she asked.

Her daughter nodded. "He treats me like I'm a real person, not just a kid to be tolerated."

Leslie realized he did that with everyone. If she could ever have invented a perfect client, Connor MacLaren was that.

Except for what he did to her senses.

She struggled toward taming them, toward becoming a professional again.

"Ready for the interview?" It was a silly question, and it sounded even sillier as she heard herself saying it. He was always ready. It was irritating that he was always so ready. Why didn't he have a fault? A wart of some kind?

"Aye," he said. "And I have tae pick up a shipment of tapes today," he added. "'Tis how I make my scones and cream."

"Scones and cream?"

"Bread and butter," he explained. "It's why my agent arranged for your agency. . . . I'm not known in Atlanta, and most of my income comes from the sale of records and tapes."

"Where are they?"

"The airport. I didna want them sent directly tae the hotel for fear they might be misplaced."

"We have time this afternoon."

"I'm monopolizing you again," he said, his expression telling her that was exactly what he had intended.

Leslie thought she should probably be vexed with him, but she couldn't be, not when he seemed so triumphant, like a boy who had just tricked a friend into doing exactly what he wanted.

"Connor . . . ?" she started.

But he easily deflected her question with one of his own, asking about the upcoming interviews, and then he slid into talking about his own schedule. The events for the Scottish Festival would begin the next day. She would attend them all, wouldn't she?

Leslie hesitated. He filled her every thought now, both day and night. And in a few days he would disappear, not in a puff of smoke but in a trail of airline vapor. Was she prepared to become more involved?

"Do you ever get tired of touring?" she finally said, trying to interject a note of reality into her wayward thoughts.

"Aye. Usually toward the end, I get homesick for Scotland, but mostly I enjoy the travel. New cities. New people. New converts for the bonniest country in the world."

"I would like to go sometime," Leslie said wistfully.

"You will," he replied with confidence, and she knew he hadn't forgotten anything about last night. No more than she had.

But she merely nodded. It was impossible. It would be impossible for the next four years, anyway. All her money was earmarked for Robin's education. There would be nothing extra for frills like traveling.

"Perhaps," she said noncommittally.

The morning sped by, just like every minute she spent in his company. He did an interview at a small independent station, and then a radio station. By noon Leslie was a bundle of nerves from spending so much time with him, from sitting close to him in the car, listening to him sing, hearing his deep chuckle. Every minute seemed to bring her closer to an explosion of some kind.

Connor insisted on selecting the restaurant for lunch, and she knew that he had done some research when he directed her to one of Atlanta's finest eateries.

But again she had no appetite and found herself picking at food as he picked at her mind.

"How long have you been in business?" he asked after fascinated stares followed them to the table.

"Seven years."

"That's quite an accomplishment . . . owning your own business."

Pleasure flooded Leslie at his obvious admiration, but honesty prompted her reply. "It's not really very large."

"But good enough to be recommended," he said. "My agent is very thorough."

"Gillian is very capable in the entertainment business."

He grinned. "And she stuck you with a folksinger?"

"I wouldn't exactly say stuck."

"Admit it, lass. That's exactly how you felt when you met my plane."

"Gillian didn't leave me a choice," she admitted.

"And your other clients? Are you neglecting them for me?"

"Never," she said. "I checked in with them yesterday, so they know I'm still alive."

"And your partner. How is she faring with her circus?"

"Oh, Gillian will prevail. She always does."

"I've been reading about the Russian circus in the paper," he said. "I think I would like her . . . rushing to the rescue of abandoned performers." He chuckled. "There's been a time or tae I could have used that kind of assistance."

Leslie couldn't believe that. He would be able to charm himself out of any situation.

"'Tis true," he claimed, obviously seeing her skeptical expression. "Once when I was in Paris, my pocket was picked. I didn't have so much as a franc."

He stopped, waiting for her to urge him to continue.

She set her chin on fist, her elbow settled firmly on the table. "Okay," she said, "let's have it."

He feigned a wounded look. "You look as if you don't believe me."

"I'm reserving judgment."

"I tried tae sing for my supper, and I was arrested. There's nothing as cold and damp as a French jail."

"And?" she prompted, fascinated.

"There was no Gillian or Leslie. I served ten days for performing without a permit. But I learned some great Parisian songs."

"With a Scottish accent?"

"It's much better than the other way round," he replied gleefully.

"And have you seen any other jails?"

"You don't want tae know, Miss Leslie," he said. "I was a feisty young cub."

"Now *that* I do believe."

"But I had a good time."

"You always have a good time," she observed.

"Ah, you noticed that, did you? I try. Life can be tae short."

But Leslie noted that his fingers tightened around the glass of beer he had ordered, and some of the laughter left his eyes.

"Do you actually live in Edinburgh?" More than anything, Leslie wanted to bring the twinkle back.

"Aye. I have a wee house not far from Edinburgh Castle."

"And when you're gone?"

"I lease it. That way my garden's tended. It's one of the conditions."

A garden was the last thing she would suspect him of having. He kept surprising her. "What kind of garden?"

"You willna tell anyone?" He gave her a half-grin.

"I swear."

"Then I'll reveal my deepest secret tae ye. Flowers."

The burr in his voice was stronger now, and she wondered whether it was because part of him was back in Scotland, in his garden. Or was he thinking about his wife and son?

"And what kind of flowers?"

He shrugged, a sheepish look on his face. "Several varieties, mainly roses."

"I never would have suspected it."

"There's something . . . restful about watching things grow," he replied as if in his own defense. "And what do you do tae enjoy yourself?"

Leslie tipped her head in thought. What *did* she do? The last few years had been consumed with her daughter and her work, in building a business. It was a lucky fluke the grass was cut occasionally, and there certainly had been no time for gardens. Or had she just not made time?

"A play, a concert, a book," she finally said.

"And what kind of plays and concerts?"

She tried to think back to the last one, a matinee she'd taken Robin to. "Musicals. *Cats, A Chorus Line*," she finally said, triumphant.

"And what else?"

There wasn't anything else, and Leslie suddenly realized there should be. Gillian had always accused her of being a hermit, of not grabbing enough from life. "There's no time," she said now, as she had said to her partner so many times. "And speaking of time . . ."

His gaze told her he knew she was using time as an excuse to change the subject. But with resignation he asked, "Where tae now?"

Their destination was a suburban daily newspaper outside of Atlanta, and then the airport, where he picked up several large packages. They were almost through now. Professionally, they were through. The Scottish Festival would officially begin tomorrow, and Leslie had no more responsibilities toward him. The thought was devastating. It robbed her of excuses. From now on, she was on her own.

No longer were they client and professional, but only man and woman. She couldn't fool herself any longer.

She drove him back to the hotel, saying she had some errands to run and calls to make.

"I'll drive over tae your home at five," he said as he untangled his long legs from the car and stepped outside, leaning over for the parting words. "For Robin's sitting. If that's all right?"

"Are you sure you have time?"

He gave her a slow, lazy grin. "I wouldna miss that for anything."

Their eyes locked. Her hands tightened on the steering wheel until they were almost white. She couldn't take her eyes from him, and she felt like a fly struggling to free itself from a spider's web.

"Have a guid afternoon," he said, the Scots accent stronger when his emotions were deeper.

She wished it didn't reverberate through her in such a harmonious way.

"Good afternoon," she said, finally putting her foot on the gas pedal. As she pulled away, she saw a charter bus unload, most of its departing passengers dressed in plaids or kilts.

He would no longer be hers alone. Robin would be present this afternoon, then the guests at the Tartan Ball on Saturday. That was all that was left.

And she already felt a terrible sense of loss.

In her wildest dreams Leslie never thought she would be feeding hamburgers to a man in a skirt in her small backyard.

But Connor sat munching happily, after sitting for Robin for thirty minutes. It had taken her daughter several minutes to take in the whole of Connor MacLaren when he presented himself. But that reaction was to be expected, Leslie thought. It had taken herself every bit as long at the airport.

Her daughter's gaze had traveled from the top of his head where he now wore a Scots bonnet—for Robin, Leslie knew—down to a pair of hose from which the handle of a dirk protruded.

Instead of a vest, he wore a jacket over a shirt and tie. He was every inch of a Scottish gentleman.

"Totally awesome, out of orbit," Robin finally said, and Leslie wondered whether that was better than "totally wow." She herself wasn't sure whether she liked Connor better in Scottish dress or in the slacks and sports coat he'd worn last night. He looked infernally handsome either way.

When Robin eyed the leather pouch at his waist, Connor said, "That's a sporran, lass. A little like your pocketbooks but a wee bit more practical. We donna have tae hold on to them."

"Do all Scotsmen wear them?" she asked.

"Aye. At dress affairs, like the ball. There will be some very fancy ones with real fur and animal heads there."

"Yech!" Robin exclaimed.

"You'll approve of mine," he said. "No head anywhere."

But her interest had already moved to a different place. "Does every Scotsman wear a dagger in his socks?"

"Hose, Robin, hose," he corrected with amusement. "Don't dare say socks tae any self-respecting Scot."

Robin giggled. "Hose sounds worse."

"Don't forget the dagger you see before you when you say that."

"*Macbeth*," Robin said.

"A somewhat fractured version. I think Mr. Shakespeare would turn over in his grave."

"But the dagger?" she persisted.

"'Tis not really a dirk but a *skene dhu*, and it's not really a weapon but a utility knife. I told you we Scots are practical."

At Robin's disappointed look he added, "But at night, to formal affairs, we wear a dirk. Does that appeal to the more bloodthirsty side of you?"

"Yep," she said.

Leslie knew he didn't need a dirk to make him more dangerous—not to her, anyway. But the Scottish attire *did* make him look more rugged, more . . . primitive. The thought caused heat to spiral through her as she remembered his kiss last night. She tried to search for the right word for him. Words were her business; she was decidedly picky about them. As she watched him talk to Robin, she thought of "elemental." Resembling a great force of nature. That certainly described him now.

What did one do with a great force of nature?

She watched as he teased Robin, and Robin took some photographs of him before sitting down with her notepad to make some sketches. Once, the girl shook her head, and Leslie recognized the problem. How do you capture on paper the essence of energy? Of exuberance? How do you transform the elemental into art?

But soon her force of nature happily accepted an offer to stay and share a dinner of hamburgers. He took off his bonnet and jacket, and started answering more of Robin's endless questions.

"The bonnet," he said, "has nothing at all in common with your Easter bonnet. It's a balmoral, and the badge on the side is that of the MacLaren clan. The shoes with the ties crossing back and forth over the open instep are 'gillie shoes.'"

Again, Robin's eyes fell to the knife at the calf of his leg. "'Twas not always innocent," he said. "Although today 'tis utilitarian, its history goes back tae the 1700s, when the English outlawed weapons and kilts after the '45 uprising, and we ha' tae find ways tae outwit them."

"And what was the uprising?" Robin wanted to know.

"Ah, that is a verrry long tale and requires a few tears in the telling," he said. "We'll leave that for another day."

And so they did, and the conversation changed to food. Rolling up his shirtsleeves, Connor demanded to cook on the small grill Leslie had outside, and she went in to hurriedly make a salad.

When she returned to the backyard, the hamburgers were well on their way to perfection, and Connor and Robin were laughing, unaware of her presence. She watched them for a moment, and her heart hurt. She hadn't really realized until now how much Robin must have missed having a father. She'd tried so hard to be both parents to her child.

"I'm being sexually harassed by your daughter," Connor said indignantly as he caught sight of Leslie.

"I only told him what great legs he has," Robin managed to say before doubling up with giggles.

"And if I told you that?" he asked sternly.

"I'd be ever so grateful." Robin retorted. Leslie looked at her usually reserved daughter with genuine amazement.

But then the hamburgers caught on fire, and both Leslie and Connor ran to rescue them. They collided, and for a moment neither could move as their bodies were pressed together for the briefest time.

Another flare and sizzle echoed the one they were experiencing.

"Mom!" Robin yelled, and Leslie whirled around. The hamburgers were engulfed in flames now. Connor grabbed a cooking tool and flipped the patties onto a plate. Leslie and Robin looked at them dubiously.

"We Scots like our meat well doon," Connor observed judiciously.

Robin giggled again, and Leslie felt her mouth crack into a smile. "Well doon, you'll have," she said.

Supper continued in the same vein of nonsense, Leslie feeling relaxed and giddy. It wasn't until they had finished eating that the physical tension between Conner and herself started to build again.

"I must go," he said regretfully. "I have an engagement tonight."

She merely nodded, not having the will to speak the appropriate words of regret.

"Will you walk me to the car?"

She nodded mutely again.

He took her hand as they walked to his rental

car. When they reached it, he took her chin in his large hand and tipped it up toward him. "It was a wonderful afternoon, Leslie."

How could hamburgers be wonderful? Especially burned ones.

"You've given something back tae me, something that has been missing these past years," he continued, possibly sensing her doubt. "Thank you."

Leslie could only stand there speechless, her heart pounding. Part of her wondered what their neighbors were thinking—Leslie Turner out here practically swooning over a man as if she were a teenager.

But Connor was apparently oblivious to such concerns. "Will you and Robin come to the Tattoo with me tomorrow night?"

She nodded, wondering whatever had happened to her power of speech.

He leaned down, his lips skimming over hers. "Hmmmmmm," he said. "You taste so good."

"Burned-hamburger cologne," she quipped, finally finding her tongue.

"As Robin says, you should bottle it." He grinned. "Tomorrow night then," he said, obviously not wanting to give her a chance to retreat. "I have tae be there early. Seven?"

She nodded again, beginning to feel like a marionette, her strings pulled by an invisible force.

"Aye," Leslie was finally able to manage.

"You're getting a fine Scottish tongue about you," he teased, and as he kissed her long and hard, Leslie discovered she didn't give a tinker's dam if everyone in the neighborhood watched.

Seven

"A taste of Scotland, love," Connor said as he led Leslie and Robin to the outdoor coliseum where the Tattoo was being held.

The familiar tingle ran up and down Leslie's backbone. She liked the way "love" sounded on his lips, the way it sort of rumbled in the air and hung there as if he didn't want to let it go.

She forced her gaze away from him and toward the colorfully dressed crowd. Leslie had never seen so many kilts in her life. More than half of the thousands of men in attendance wore full Scots regalia, and many of the women were in kilts or plaids of some type. Nor had she ever heard so many swirling bagpipes warming up in practice. It was an eerie sound in the cool, clear night in Atlanta. Stone Mountain was, indeed, a piece of Scotland tonight.

Did this remind Connor of home? Of his family? Of a life so different from her own?

The evening itself was magical. A full harvest moon sat complacently in the sky, and a nip in the air was just enough to whet the senses.

Not that they needed whetting.

Whenever Connor was within the general proximity, her senses were about as whetted as they could be.

Connor kept her and Robin close to him, drawing them to a section for special guests. He would be performing later, he said, but in the meantime he would stay with them.

Leslie felt incredibly special when he leaned his dark head down toward her, giving her his full attention as he pointed out the guest of honor, an earl, and several other dignitaries.

"An earl, a real earl?" Robin exclaimed. Leslie was surprised that her daughter, who was usually blasé about anything social, even cared.

"Aye," he said with a twinkle. "And clan chief too."

"I think it would be great to be part of a clan," Robin said.

"You probably are, someplace back. A wee part of you, anyway. A number of Americans are."

Robin looked at Leslie. "Mom?"

Leslie nodded. "Yep. My grandfather was half Scotch-Irish. That makes you . . . one sixteenth Scottish."

Robin looked at Connor. "Does that count?"

"As good as any," he answered as he turned to Leslie. "What was the name."

"Grant."

"Ah, a very fine Scots name," he said, and Robin beamed.

"In fact," he said, "I think I see a Grant over there." He leaned over and pointed out a man in the guest section.

"Do you know *everyone*?" Robin asked, a little awed.

"There's a number of people who go tae more than one festival during the year," he replied. "You get tae know them."

Perhaps not everyone would. But Connor would. She'd already discovered he had a phenomenal memory for names and faces. And it wasn't all business. He remembered because he liked people and found something interesting in each one.

"You should be in politics," Leslie said.

"Are you trying tae tell me something about my music?" he teased.

"Only that you have more than one talent."

"Ah," he whispered in a voice meant only for her. "I hope I do." His tone made the implication quite clear, and Leslie felt herself tingling inside, with something suspiciously like desire.

She glanced quickly at Robin to see whether she had heard anything, but Robin's attention was now directed toward the field. She had brought along a sketch pad and was drinking in all the sights, her eyes bright with the same excitement that seemed to be affecting everyone.

Leslie understood. There was so much color here, so much atmosphere.

"Just wait," Connor whispered to them both. "I never get tired of this."

As hundreds of musicians, over half of them bearing bagpipes and drums, marched into the arena, she understood what he meant. There was a grandeur about the spectacle, and she felt an unexpected surge of blood at the sound of hundreds of bagpipes in unison. She wondered if there was a bit of Scotland lurking deep down inside everyone.

Her hand had become locked with his, and she increased the pressure of her grip. "It's wonderful," she told him.

Some of the joy left her when he took his leave just before the intermission. She knew he was on the program, and she had bittersweet feelings about it: A sense of pride and also of déjà vu.

When he started singing alone in the middle of the field, his voice amplified by electronic gear, the noisy, enthusiastic crowd hushed.

Leslie recognized some of the songs, and she had heard enough interviews to know the stories behind them. Robin's hand caught hers when he sang the "Skye Boat Song" and "These Are My Mountains," and the crowd erupted with cheers and claps when he finished with "Scotland the Brave."

She was struck by the phrase "one shining moment." That's the way she felt now, with pride and something close to love swelling inside her as Connor MacLaren transported the crowd to another time, another place. She'd had several shining moments with him, but that was all there was, all there could be.

As the applause roared over the stands, she remembered another time, another place, where applause also rang. All the pleasure in her dissolved into pain—pure, inconsolable agony. Shining moments were like tin that was plated with silver—deceptive.

Leslie looked down at her daughter, whose face was as transformed as those around them. Had she just set Robin up for a very long and hard fall? Had she done that to herself as well?

He didn't come right back. She saw bands taking the field and caught sight of him in a crowd, signing programs. He occasionally darted a glance toward her, but then would bend his head, listening to whoever was speaking. As Tommy had once, though he'd never bothered to acknowledge her existence at such times. It ruined his image, he'd told her.

What was she doing? Repeating the worst mistake in her life?

Tommy had been dead for twelve years. It might as well have been eighteen. On the day she had told him she was pregnant, her husband had walked out of her life for good. He didn't want to be saddled with a baby, or even a wife anymore. He was at the height of his success then, the lead singer with one of the top rock groups, and he never sent her a penny for Robin's support. His . . . bodyguards shielded him from calls, and court orders went unheeded. He spent everything on alcohol and drugs. Four years after their divorce she'd learned about his drug-overdose death from a national tabloid. There was nothing left as far as financial assets, only debt, including a whopping one to Uncle Sam.

And now Connor MacLaren. The same dynamics pushed both of them, Tommy and Connor—crowds, applause.

She wasn't aware that tears had formed at the corners of her eyes until Robin's voice penetrated. "Are you all right, Mom?"

"Of course, love," she answered as lightly as possible. "It's just the music."

Robin was silent for a moment. "He's very good, isn't he?"

Leslie nodded.

"I like him a lot."

"Don't like him too much, Robin. He'll be leaving Sunday."

"He could come back."

Leslie shook her head. "He has his own life."

"I think he really likes you."

"I think he likes everyone," Leslie said.

Robin shrugged, but there was disbelief in her face.

When Connor returned, she moved a little closer to Robin, creating an invisible barrier between herself and Connor. Her hands busied themselves with the program. He gave her a quizzical look, as if he recognized her maneuvering but didn't understand it.

"You were super," Robin said, breaking the silence.

His mouth twitched mischievously. "I like your vocabulary."

Their next words were swallowed by music. Five different bagpipe groups were playing a medley of Scottish melodies, and dancers had entered the field.

"The sword dance," Connor whispered to her. The dancers had lain down their swords in an X and were stepping quickly between the steel blades. The dance required wonderful precision, and Leslie tried to focus her attention on the performers, hoping to minimize the impact of the man next to her.

And then she felt his own withdrawal, a kind of surrender, and she wondered at the emptiness she felt.

Why can't you accept these days, these hours, for what they are? A fleeting piece of time that you can remember and treasure. Why make a major trauma out of it?

Because it was already major, she answered herself. Her heart was already involved, her soul committed, despite all the warnings.

And it terrified her.

The theme song from the movie *Chariots of Fire* penetrated her consciousness. She remembered the film. It was about a commitment and never giving up. She felt her hand move away from the program, which had been clenched tightly between her fists, and come to rest on Connor's kilt. His hand quickly took it, the big fist swallowing hers, the hard fingers pressing tightly as if he, too, had suddenly sensed loss.

She looked up at him with eyes she knew spoke volumes. She wished again she could express her feelings, but something prevented it.

"Something wrong, love?" There it was again. That wonderful word that made her quake inside.

She shook her head. "I'll just miss this." *Miss you, and that's something I don't want to do.*

"We'll fill you full of Scottish music during the next three days," he said. "You'll be full tired of it by Sunday."

She hoped so, but she knew differently. Besides it wasn't the music that she wanted. "I wonder," she whispered under her breath.

But he either heard her or read her thoughts. "I'll think of some kind of solution. . . ." She sensed a promise, one that frightened even as it made her hope.

She shivered, and Connor shrugged off his coat and put it around her shoulders. It smelled so distinctly of him, of that particularly masculine scent that somehow brought images of rugged Scottish mountains. She wondered whether she would ever forget it.

And then the Tattoo was over, and one of Connor's arms went around her in a possessive way, while the other dropped protectively on Robin's shoulder. Leslie saw surprise dart across her daughter's face and then a grin of delight replaced it. She shivered again, and his arm tightened and pulled her closer as he maneuvered them out and toward the car that was parked nearby. He nodded to people but didn't stop, and Leslie had the impression of a very determined steamroller.

So did everyone else, apparently, because they parted like the Red Sea before him.

When they reached Leslie's home, Robin nearly bounced out of the car, giving Leslie a knowing stare. "School tomorrow," she said, although that had never been a priority with her.

Before Leslie could follow her, Connor had her hand, imprisoning her. "You'll not be running away from me again."

"I have to work tom—"

The last word was silenced by his lips. The

shining moments returned, and they definitely were not tin, she thought before she lost every one of her reservations.

His need reached deep into her very vulnerable emotions. His lips opened her mouth, and his tongue probed slowly but insistently, awakening an eager response and spurring it until she was as much the aggressor as he.

His hands gently traced patterns along the back of her neck, and the very lightness of the touch made them erotic. Leslie's every nerve ending tingled with expectancy, and she was filled with an aching hunger as his lips moved from her mouth to her neck with scorching thoroughness. "You feel so guid," he whispered. The cadence of his speech, now endearingly familiar to her, seemed to hum in the cool air within the car.

Her fingers climbed upward, catching locks of his dark hair, and she felt him tense, just as she had. The air in the car was charged now, pregnant with mutual need.

Leslie felt herself tremble in his arms, wanting the warmth of him, the giving that radiated from him.

His mouth felt so wonderful as his lips played against hers, fondling, loving, teasing. Every part of her body ached and quivered and strained toward him as she met kiss for kiss. She savored the taste of him when his tongue entered her mouth and played games with every sense she knew she had and some she didn't.

His hand went to one of her breasts, touching but still not demanding. Every move had been tentative, questioning, as if he were afraid she might disappear.

"I donna know what's happening, Leslie," he whispered, "but something sure as the devil is. I canna get you out of my mind."

"I know," she said softly, finally admitting to

him, to herself, that something indeed was happening.

He cradled her against his chest, then her chin was slowly tilted up by one strong hand until she was looking directly into his eyes. He kissed her again, slowly and lingeringly. When his lips parted from her, a hand remained touching her face as if he couldn't bear to lose contact.

She straightened, stiffening against him, against herself.

"What's wrong, love?" he said slowly. "You keep backing away."

I don't want to. I really don't want to, but I'm so afraid of being hurt. The words were there in her mind, but she couldn't say them. It would be revealing the hurt and humiliation she'd felt for years.

But she might as well have, for she heard him whisper, "The bastard. Whoever he was, he's a bloody bastard."

There was deep anger in the words, and Leslie felt the cloak of protection. She hadn't realized how much she needed it. She had steeled herself all these years against the wounds and the memories, the sense of unworthiness that Tommy had left as his legacy. She thought she had defeated it, but now she knew she hadn't.

It had been hiding somewhere, a dark shadow ready to pounce when she started to open her heart again.

To her chagrin, she felt tears gathering in her eyes, felt one begin a wandering path down her cheek. Leslie felt a burning embarrassment.

"Ah, don't, love," he said. The word *love* rolled off his tongue, and it was the most comforting sound she'd ever heard.

The tears magically stopped as if they had heard and obeyed. When she looked up at him, she thought she'd feel foolish, but she felt only a sense of bonding with him, a kind of belonging.

"Would you tell me about him?"

She shook her head. She wasn't ready yet. No matter how much Connor had touched her in the past few days, he was still in many ways a stranger. And he would be gone in three more days.

The thought was devastating.

"I think I'd better go inside," she said. "But thank you. It was a lovely evening. Robin loved it."

"And you?"

"I loved it too," she admitted.

"I know I'm monopolizing your time," he said, "but there's a reception tomorrow night. Would you go with me?"

"And Robin too?"

There was the barest hesitancy. "If she'd like."

"But it's more for adults?"

"Aye," he said. "I don't really think she'd enjoy it that much."

She nodded, accepting his observation. "She asked me what she should wear to the Tartan Ball."

He smiled then, that wonderfully full smile that included the world in its warmth. "I have a wee surprise for you both," he said with satisfaction. "It should be delivered tomorrow."

Leslie thought she should protest, but he looked so darned pleased with himself, she couldn't. "I *would* like to go tomorrow night," she found herself saying instead.

Connor suffered through the next day. His thoughts constantly turned to Leslie. She was like the will-o'-the-wisp, one moment with him, the next gone.

He didn't understand her or himself. He had

never pursued anyone like this before, and deep inside he knew how unwise it was. He could do nothing but hurt them both.

Leslie had made it obvious that trusting did not come easily to her. She had been hurt, and hurt badly; that was very clear.

And he had his own past to deal with. He knew he wasn't ready for marriage again, not until he could settle down, and that time hadn't come yet.

They were two people who should never have met and, once they did, should have stayed a million miles away from each other.

Yet, as much as he tried, he couldn't do it. His mouth had asked her questions his mind warned him not to speak, and his kisses made promises he knew he couldn't keep.

Leslie with the moss-green eyes. Leslie with the competence and yet the vulnerability that touched him as nothing else could. Leslie, who made him feel alive and giving. It was the giving that felt so good, so damnably good.

And he was terribly afraid that in the giving, he would take.

Yet, he kept asking the questions, like a lemming going to its own destruction.

Thank heaven for normal clients like Steven Morrow and his development and grand opening.

Those things forced Leslie to concentrate the next day. She knew, perhaps more than anyone, how much this development meant to her client.

She had an appointment with him at ten, and she'd prepared several press releases for his approval. They also went over the celebrity golf tournament, Leslie making several suggestions for possible guests, and then they reviewed the preliminary sketch for the full-page advertisement scheduled for the daily paper. Three hours passed before they finished, and Leslie wasn't completely satisfied. There was something missing from the plans, but she couldn't put her finger on it. Yet Steve was pleased, and so she felt she should be too.

A package was on Leslie's doorstep when she arrived home, and only then did she remember what Connor had said last night about a "wee surprise."

She opened it and found two long gowns, both lovely in their simplicity. One was white with a sash she recognized as the same plaid as Connor's kilt. The other was a very light green with a similar plaid. She looked at the sizes. The light green was a ten, her size, and the white an eight. The realization that he had a very good eye for sizes gave her a moment's pause, but she pushed it aside.

Her hand caressed the fine cloth, and then she ran upstairs to try on the green dress. In the full-length mirror, she had the odd feeling of being transported back into another century. Was that really Leslie Turner staring back at her? Her figure looked graceful and enticingly rounded, and the green and blue in the plaid complimented her coloring, deepening the green in her eyes.

She whirled around, watching as the flared skirt moved with her. Cinderella. She felt just like Cinderella.

A thirty-seven-year-old Cinderella, she reminded herself. A jaded Cinderella. A Cinderella who was a mother and should know better.

Just the same, she wouldn't have been a bit surprised if a real carriage and horses called for her.

Eight

"As Robin would say, totally terrific," Connor said as Leslie opened the door that evening. "Or, something like that. I don't know whether I've mastered American teenage dialect."

Leslie winced. "Don't even try. I like 'bonny' and 'lass' and 'tae' much better."

He sighed with mock relief. "You look very bonny then."

Pleasure surged through Leslie. She had spent hours shopping this afternoon, but Connor's appreciation made the time well spent.

He'd leaned over and kissed her, the caress spontaneous and lingering until they heard Robin's voice coming from the top of the stairs.

"Is that Connor or Denny?"

"Denny?" Connor asked.

"Denise. Her best friend. She's going to spend the night with her tonight."

The words slipped out before Leslie could halt them. She hadn't really meant to impart that information, not until she was sure that she really wanted him to know they could, would, have privacy tonight.

If he realized the significance of the words, he

didn't indicate it. His face turned instead toward the stairs from which Robin was descending, dressed again in a raggedy pair of jeans and a painted T-shirt.

"The dress you sent is really neat," she said, "and you should see Mom in hers!"

He grinned. "I plan tae."

"Of course, I don't dare let my friends see it," she continued in a breezy, teasing fashion.

"Totally unwow?" he asked, his face creasing with amusement as he winked at Leslie.

"Me in a dress?" Robin confided. "Outer space happening."

"You'll be the prettiest lass there."

"What about Mom?" she asked shyly.

"One of the tae prettiest lasses there," he corrected himself.

"And you'll really teach me those dances?"

He bowed royally. "It will be my pleasure."

A car horn blew from outside. "That's Denny. See ya later." She practically flew out the door, stopping midway and turning back. "Have fun," she yelled, then was gone.

"She's a bit of a whirlwind," he observed as the door slammed behind her.

"Among other things," Leslie said with resignation. "It's never dull, but having a seventeen-year-old can age you quickly."

"Or keep you young," he added a bit wistfully.

"Hmmmm," she said dubiously.

"She's an enchanting girl."

"She can be, yes," Leslie agreed. "In fact, most of the time she is. But she can also be reckless."

"Is that an inherited trait?" His hand caught hers and pulled her close to him.

"I didn't used to think so."

His head lowered, and his lips closed down on hers. Responding in a way that proved she had indeed turned reckless, she met him readily this time. Her tongue played with his, exploring as deeply as he did, letting every emotion simmer and boil until her legs felt hollow, as if they would collapse under her.

But then his hands caught her behind her back, pressing her to him, and she felt every bit of his rock-hard manhood under the kilt he was wearing. Scorching heat crawled up and down her midsection, and her body clung to him in the most needy way.

It was only by pure force of will that she was able to move back, away from the danger, from the overwhelming want within her, and she knew, looking downward, that she wasn't the only one feeling the force of desire. There was some things even a kilt couldn't hide.

Her voice was a little shaky when she said, "I suppose . . . we should go. It would probably be nice if the guests of honor appeared."

He followed the direction of her gaze, and his expression turned wry. "Like this?"

"Aye," she said, surprised by the laughter she could barely contain.

"Ye hae tae promise tae behave." She had never heard his Scots accent so pronounced, and she wondered what that indicated.

"I'll do my very best," she said, taking his hand and drawing him toward the door.

"You're a heartless soul."

"Aye," she said again, feeling as young as a filly in a rich green pasture.

But when they arrived at Stone Mountain Park for the Sponsors' Reception, all the realities flooded back. They were at once mobbed by Connor's friends and fans, and Leslie found herself backing more and more into a mental corner.

She remembered some of the faces from the guest stand at the Tattoo, but there were many others she didn't recognize. The names were mostly

Scottish—McDonald, Mcleod, McAfee, McKay, McMillian, Mckenzie, McPherson, and Murray. They all started to blur together in her mind, as did the faces. Whiskey flowed like water, and so did the conversation. Many of the accents were similar to Connor's, their rhythm and cadence carrying through the air like a song.

Leslie sipped a cup of wine while Connor nursed a glass of whiskey, though he was urged to do otherwise by many of those who came by to drink a toast with him.

As his natural ebullience reached out and touched everyone, Leslie felt the uncomfortable bite of jealousy. She didn't like it, didn't like what it signified, but neither would it go away. So she stood and nodded and uttered meaningless words.

And finally, it was over. She was silent on the way home, though he had taken her hand and drew her to him. Leslie felt the electricity of his body, the magnetic pull between the two of them. The house was empty, and she knew, deep down, that she was glad. Yet she was scared too. She wasn't sure she was ready for this kind of commitment.

Leslie had not gone to bed with anyone since her marriage. There had been many reasons, but basically she felt physical intimacy went with love and was not to be entered into lightly. She had dated, though infrequently, and she knew most of her dates thought she had dinosaur-age beliefs.

But now her body ached to be touched and held. A craving deep inside was proliferating, spreading like wildfire until every one of her nerves tingled with expectation. She saw from the tenseness of Connor's body that he felt the same.

The first time she'd seen him, she'd wondered what Scotsmen wore under their kilts. She knew she was going to find out tonight.

Leslie was scarcely aware of the drive home.

Almost in a trance she allowed Connor to go around and open her car door and take her hand, rather than springing up and out as she had several times earlier.

His touch was full of reassurance, as if he understood every one of her reservations. But how could he? He paused just inside of the door, pulling her to him. "I've been wanting tae do this all evening," he whispered just before his lips came down on hers, hard this time, and demanding and even a bit desperate.

The lump in her stomach disappeared. The caution fled. The reservations vanished.

Nothing mattered now but Connor MacLaren.

Nothing but Connor and the wonderful sensations flooding her.

Nothing but the tender violence of a kiss that combined longing and raw need.

Connor's mouth moved hungrily, his tongue inviting her to join with him, spreading a honeyed, wheedling warmth throughout her body. The warmth became heat and then fever as her body melded into his.

Leslie heard the rapid beat of his heart, and she found her hands moving to the back of his neck, teasing with whisper-soft strokes. As her hands moved, so did her tongue, meeting his with equal hunger until they were both caught in frantic eddies of desire that couldn't be stopped.

His mouth moved from hers, and brushed over her cheek, his lips skimming along the edge of her face to the nape of her neck, inciting every nerve ending, every feeling part of her, until she thought she would burst with the pressure building within her.

She felt his manhood swell against her, and the craving inside grew stronger, more insistent.

Connor's lips found her ear, nuzzling the lobe gently, stroking with his tongue its most sensitive part. Her breath quickened, her hands becoming more aggressive.

Her eyes met his, and the exchange between them needed no words.

Are you sure?

No. She wasn't sure, but that didn't make any difference. She was being sucked inexorably into a vortex that allowed no escape but one.

"Yes," she whispered.

His hand went to her chin, fondling it as if giving her one more chance, even while they both knew there were no other choices.

Leslie took his hand, leading him upstairs to her bedroom, and she saw his gaze wander over the hardwood floors partially covered by a hook rug dominated by rose colors, and matching curtains and quilt. Leslie had always thought it a tranquil room, but at that moment there was nothing restful about its charged atmosphere.

Connor's hands undressed her, loving her as he did so, each touch a caress in its own right. She trembled at the feelings he aroused—tumultuous, swelling, raging feelings.

Leslie found herself undressing him, her hands shrugging off his jacket, unknotting the tie he wore, undoing the buttons on his shirt. She wasn't sure what to do about the kilt, and she stood back, savoring the glimpse of hard, broad shoulders and chest under his now-half-open shirt as she took the sporran from his waist and then unbuckled his belt. Once again, she reveled at the pure masculinity of the male form in a kilt.

His hands deftly undid two straps that obviously loosened the kilt, and it started to drop away from him, his hands catching it easily. His shirt was long, falling below his hips, but she saw immediately what Scots did not wear under their kilts.

Connor looked at her and grinned. "It's quite true, you see," he said, as if reading her mind.

Leslie found herself grinning too. "I didn't believe it. Don't you feel . . . drafty?"

He roared. "Certainly nae at the moment," he said. "And Scots used tae go into battle totally naked. I think the theory was it would scare the bloody English tae death."

"Did it work?"

"I donna know," he replied with a wink. "But when we became proper, 'twas only then the English seemed tae get the upper hand."

Leslie knew she *didna* care about the English at the moment, not when Connor shrugged off the long-tailed linen shirt and stood as tall and strong as the men he sang about. At the same time she realized the Scots might have had a wee bit of a point all those hundreds of years before. An army of naked Connors would be enough to dazzle and blind a hundred armies.

He gave her no time to consider the matter further. He moved toward her, and as his hands finished undressing her, his mouth claimed her lips. "You are a lovely lass," he said softly.

His hands dipped suddenly into the sporran, then for a few moments he busied himself with a foil packet. And then they were both on the bed, and Leslie felt his body strain toward her. His fingers moved slowly, exquisitely along the side of her breasts, finally cupping them as his mouth came down and played with nipples grown hard with passion.

Surges of physical delight swamped her. She gasped at the feelings he aroused—swelling, wondrous feelings that pushed her body to his in response.

His manhood touched and played and teased against her as the tension and expectation grew and she ached for relief. A gnawing craving overwhelmed her; she desperately wanted him to become a part of her.

All the time, his hands caressed, soothing while burning, reassuring while inciting. Her body was so unused to these sensations that they were all shiny new—new and incredibly delicious. Had she ever felt this way with Tommy? She didn't think so—not this tender giving rather than rough taking. She hadn't realized then that loving could be a gentle thing.

But that was exactly what Connor was making it. Gentle and wonderful, yet so sensuous and . . . and glorious. Something wild and primal surged through her, and her hands clasped his back, bringing him to her fiercely, as possessively as he had kissed her earlier.

Leslie felt his warmth enter her, and she stifled a cry. It had been so long, and she was so tight, but then sensations overwhelmed her as he moved, slowly at first and then with more urgency. Yet he never hurried, obviously restraining himself to bring her with him every step. She gasped with the growing intensity of the sensations rocking her, as he plunged deeper and deeper in great shuddering movements, each one creating waves of such ecstasy that she could hardly bear them. . . .

Yet her body kept seeking, as did his. She found herself reacting in a way she'd never expected, moving in intimate exotic dances, her body melding with his in equal fervor, in a kind of equality in which they both gave and took and explored and relished doing so. The sensations built and built until, shuddering, he exploded in her, and she collapsed in hundreds of tingling vibrations.

She felt him quiet inside her as he held her tightly, his lips touching hers in almost awed reverence as his body shuddered with tremors from the aftermath.

"So much fire," he whispered, as his lips glazed hers.

She looked up at him. "I never even realized it before."

He was silent, his hands caressing her in that possessive way she was learning to expect. "Robin's father?"

She sensed he had been wanting to ask the question before. After all, he had told her about his marriage, at least a little. And she liked the way he phrased it. Not "your husband," but "Robin's father," as if he didn't want to think of him in terms of his relationship with Leslie. The thought pleased her

She shook her head in answer to his unspoken question. No, Tommy had never aroused her the way Connor had tonight. She wondered now whether she had been in love with an image. When she met Tommy, she had been so young— only seventeen—and easily awed by him, then already a minor star.

"He just always took," she said.

Connor's fingers played tenderly along hers. "You said he died."

"A drug overdose," she answered steadily. "Years ago."

A muscle throbbed slightly in his cheek. "I'm sorry."

"He'd left us long before that, just after I learned I was pregnant." But as she said the words, the pain was gone. For the first time, it was gone.

She was grateful that he asked no more questions, but his hold on her tightened.

Leslie snuggled down against him, thinking what a luxury it was. She hadn't known how good it was to be so physically close to someone, to share such intimate feelings.

"You feel so good," she sighed contentedly.

"So do you, love," he replied. He very lightly massaged the side of her face with the back of his hand. "I donna think I ever want tae leave."

"But you will. You have to," she said softly, almost willing him to make the words a lie.

He was silent for a moment, and when he finally spoke it was with a wistful resignation. "Aye."

At least he didn't pretend, he didn't lie, Leslie thought. But at the moment she half-wished he had, for she felt such emptiness overwhelm her, she thought she might be sucked into it. She started to move away from him.

"Donna go," he commanded in a voice lower than usual.

Leslie hesitated, knowing the longer she stayed in his arms, the more difficult it would be to give him up.

"I have tae leave on Sunday," he continued, his tone more intense, "but I will come back, Leslie."

She wished she could believe him, but she knew how many distractions there were on a tour. She was one right now—could she really be different from the others?

"Leslie," he said again. "Listen tae me. I *will* come back. And perhaps you can come tae Scotland. I canna, willna, gi' you up."

His hands were running up and down her arms now, igniting little brush fires wherever they moved. He leaned down, and his lips touched the lobe of her ear, his tongue sending sensuous messages she couldn't refuse.

Leslie found her hands moving around him, her fingers tangling themselves in his thick, dark hair.

I canna, willna, gi' you up.

Leslie wasn't sure she believed him, but she wanted to. How badly she wanted to!

And then his lips found hers. And it didn't make any difference whether she believed or not.

He left at dawn. Today—Saturday—was the opening of the Scottish Festival at the park, and he was scheduled for performances throughout the day.

She had made some coffee; he'd declined anything more.

He leaned against the counter, sipping his coffee. He looked roguish with the start of a beard on his cheeks. He had dressed, but the shirt was unbuttoned at the top. He had donned the kilt again, and she'd found the garment even more appealing, now that she knew what it covered.

"You'll come today," he said, his eyes intent on her.

Leslie had nodded helplessly. She had discovered in the past week that she could deny him nothing. She'd even stopped trying. She had two more days. Hours, really . . . hours filled with other people. Selfishly, she begrudged every second he would spend with them.

"I think Robin wants to bring her friend with her."

"I'll watch for them," he said, "and sing them a song."

"Robin will love that."

"And I'll sing you a song."

"You already have," she said, trying to sound casual.

He turned serious. "I meant what I said last night. I canna let you go."

Leslie turned away from him to pour more coffee into her own cup.

"Leslie?"

Her hand shook slightly, and the hot brew spilled over onto her hands. The cup fell, the ceramic cracking and the liquid spilling everywhere.

She looked down at the robe she was wearing. It had been a present from Robin, an extravagant one, and now it was pockmarked with ugly dark stains. Tears gathered at the corner of her eyes, and it wasn't altogether because of the robe. All the safety she had thought she'd built, provided for herself and Robin, now seemed like quicksand. Every time she moved, she seemed to sink deeper in the morass of caring, of wanting, of reaching for something that was just beyond her.

The robe was symbolic of that, suddenly.

She looked up from the robe and noticed that Connor had moved toward her, his face more serious than she'd seen it, his eyes steady and intense. His hand took her chin and lifted it until she had to gaze directly at him.

She had known him five days, and as she watched him now, it seemed so much longer. As if she had known him forever, as if he'd become a permanent part of her life.

"Sometimes I'm much better at singing songs than saying words," he said. "But the ones I do say I mean. Last night was very special, and I donna intend tae let you go. I didna plan for this tae happen, but I donna think there was any way of preventing it either."

"I . . ." Leslie stopped. She didn't know what she wanted to say. She didn't even know exactly how she felt about promises, or long-distance romances.

But he took any answer away from her. He put one finger on her mouth as if he were afraid of what she might say. "Not now," he said. "Tonight." He leaned down and kissed her very hard. "Thank you."

And then he was gone.

But his presence still filled the house and—Leslie knew—her heart. And she was so afraid he was going to break it.

Nine

Connor couldn't ever remember being late before.
Not for a performance.

It had taken every ounce of control he had to
leave Leslie this morning. She had looked so
incredibly uncertain and vulnerable. And the expression had been particularly agonizing since he
knew how competent and sure of herself she
usually was.

He remembered her laughter at lunch a few
days earlier, and again last night. There was a
vein of joy in her somewhere, but it had been
boarded up and buried. He didn't know why,
exactly, but he knew that it had happened.

More than anything else, he wanted to uncover
it, to see it glow. He saw her as an older Robin,
carefree and ebullient and full of hope.

She had been that way for a time last night. She
had laughed and played and teased, and he'd
been captivated. And then the curtain had closed
again.

It had something to do with her husband. He
knew that. He had wanted to ask her about him.
He couldn't imagine a man who would leave Leslie
and a child. He would have sold his soul for

Douglas, given his own life, if he could have, in exchange for his son's life.

He had wanted to ask, but he hadn't. He had ghosts of his own he couldn't share yet, and he hadn't wanted to press Leslie when her eyes had clouded so.

He had also made promises he hadn't meant to make. But as he said them, he knew he would keep them.

Connor had realized then that he loved her. He didn't know how such overwhelming feelings could develop in such a short time, but he knew they had. He felt whole again, as he hadn't in years. He liked just being with her, just looking at those clear, determined green eyes. He liked her strength and her vulnerability and the tenderness she aroused in him.

The tenderness and the passion.

He took a shower and shaved quickly after he arrived at the hotel, changing to a full-sleeve linen shirt with an open neck with lacings, and a brown leather vest. He also put on another kilt and a fresh pair of kilt hose, tucking in the dagger. He grabbed his guitar and left, hoping that the arrangements he'd made to sell the tapes and records were in place. He'd never before left so many loose ends.

He needed to get his mind back on business. It just bloody well wouldn't cooperate.

Halfway out the door, he paused, then strode to the telephone and called Leslie's number. The line was busy. He swore briefly, looked at the telephone as if it were an offending beast, then hurried out.

Leslie paced the living room floor of her house restlessly as she waited for Robin and Denise.

She had tried to erase all signs that she'd had

an overnight visitor, but she felt the fact was imprinted on her face like a scarlet letter.

You're a grown modern lady, she told herself, but that hadn't erased the twinges of guilt. She had lectured Robin repeatedly on the advantages of waiting for marriage or, at the very least, love. She didn't know how much of her advice was taken; she wondered if any mother ever did, but she hated the feeling of being hypocritical.

But was it hypocritical? She *was* in love. She had known that last night, but would Robin realize that? She'd known Connor less than one week. Robin obviously liked him, but she believed him only a casual visitor.

It was incredibly foolish of her to fall in love, Leslie chided herself. But it felt so altogether wonderful and right. Even now, her heart was singing a song of its own, and warmth coiled deep inside at the thought of seeing him soon.

The phone rang, and she ran for it. It was Gillian. She would probably be in Boston another four or five days. She had won the release of the animals, but now she had to find a way of getting them to Georgia—free. How was Connor MacLaren? Had the interviews gone all right? Had it been too much of an imposition? Didn't Leslie like him?

As usual, Gillian's questions ran together, giving Leslie no time to answer one before the next came. When her partner had finally run out of breath, Leslie answered one by one. "Fine. Yes. No. Yes."

There was a pause on the other end. "I forgot my own questions."

Leslie ran through them patiently, trying to keep any additional information from imparting through her tone of voice. She didn't want Gillian to make assumptions. Once this week was over . . . "Mr. MacLaren is fine. . . ."

"Mr. . . . ?"

"He's a client, Gilly." Even Leslie winced at the too-proper tone in her voice. And the hypocrisy behind it. For the second time today.

There was a pause, and then with what could be disappointment, "You don't like him."

All of a sudden Leslie wondered whether Gillian had planned the whole thing. But she couldn't have. Even Gillian couldn't have started the progression of events that had sent her to Boston. But that didn't mean she hadn't taken advantage of them. Leslie hesitated, then spoke. "Of course I like him. Who wouldn't?"

"And that's all?" The disappointment was now obvious.

"He's leaving tomorrow, Gilly," Leslie said flatly.

"He seemed great on the telephone, and his agent said he was easy to work with," Gillian said, following her own train of thought.

"The agent was right, and now tell me what's happening there?"

The question took Gillian's mind away from Connor as was intended, and she talked for several minutes about the distraught chimpanzee, traumatized trick dogs, and other animals she'd obviously fallen in love with. Gillian loved animals as much as she loved causes. She had a dog and cat of her own, both now being tended by her landlady.

Just as Leslie hung up, Robin and Denise stormed noisily into the house. "We're ready, Mom," Robin said. "Denny doesn't believe how great Connor is. Are you ready? He did promise us a song, didn't he? Come on, Denny, I'll show you my dress. It's, like, out of orbit."

The screen door was still slamming as the two girls disappeared up the steps. Lauren grinned to herself as she took one last look in the mirror. Robin and Denise would keep her mind occupied for the next few moments, but once they arrived at the park, she had a feeling they would take off like two shots from a cannon.

As they walked to the fields where the festival was taking place, they were assaulted by sounds. Bagpipe music was coming from every direction: Bands on the field, individuals warming up, recordings blaring from the tented shops located nearly everywhere. On the left, muscular young men on the athletic field were throwing what looked like telephone poles. To the right, military groups were marching on a field.

Robin and Denise came to an absolute stop as they caught sight of the athletic games, their eyes growing wide at the muscular perfection of young male bodies clad in kilts and white linen shirts whose sleeves were rolled up to the forearm.

"Why don't we meet you later?" Robin said. Denise seemed suddenly rooted to the ground.

"I thought you wanted to see Connor."

"He's going to be singing all day, isn't he?"

"Off and on at the Expo Stage," Leslie answered as she eyed Robin's pleading expression. She looked down at her watch. "I'll meet you there at noon."

"Great," Robin said, and moved next to Denise as a young man in a kilt picked up a telephone pole as if it were no more than a small piece of kindling wood.

When Leslie arrived at the Expo Stage, there was an unfamiliar couple performing, and nearly every chair was taken. It was only then she realized how empty she felt at not seeing Connor instantly, and how much worse it would be in the coming days. She suspected she would never again stop looking for a kilt, or listening for his deep baritone voice.

"I was afraid you wouldna come."

The voice was there. And so was the kilt. The dark hair. And the joy he brought to her heart.

"I had to wait for Robin."

"And where is she?"

"Admiring Scottish athletes with her friend."

"She's never seen men throw logs before? Such a deprived childhood."

He sounded so regretful, Leslie had to laugh. "She's making up for it now."

He smiled at her, his lips looking impossibly sensuous, now that she had tasted them in every possible way. She wanted to do it again. Right there and then.

Sensible, conservative Leslie, she thought drolly. Well, both of those attributes were gone with the wind. Gone with the tempest that whirled around an irresistible Scots folksinger.

"I have a few hours tae make up for myself," Connor said. "I've missed you this morning."

I'll miss you all my life. She was afraid the thought showed shamelessly in her eyes, because he took her hand in his.

Leslie was only faintly aware of the milling crowds, of the sprightly tune now coming from the stage, of the leaves falling around her. She was aware only of the heat that always seemed to surround them, of the brightness in Connor's eyes, even more brilliant than the clear autumn sky above.

"Mr. MacLaren." A determined voice shattered the momentary spell that surrounded them, and Leslie forced her gaze from his face and toward a woman waiting to speak to him, her hands holding a program and pen. "Would you sign this for me?" The look on her face was of total adoration.

Leslie stumbled backward. *Will you sign this for me?* How many times had she heard that years ago? How many times had Tommy disappeared shortly afterward? Could she go through something like that again? Could Robin?

She had spent her life trying to protect Robin from the truth about her father. Her daughter knew that he had died from a drug overdose. Curious about her father, she had gone to the library and searched out clippings about him. But Leslie had never told her about the womanizing. She had told Robin it had been the pressure of always trying to stay on top that had caused him to take drugs. But that hadn't been the problem at all; Tommy had just never grown up, had been like a kid in the candy store, and everyone was eager to serve him. The one time he was refused, he resorted to extremes: He'd married.

Leslie turned blindly around. Connor wasn't anything like Tommy, she told herself. Her husband had never had the maturity or self-confidence that Connor did.

But Connor had said his wife died years ago, and he had apparently never married again. Because he liked the road? Enjoyed the freedom it gave him?

"Leslie." She felt his hand clasp hers. "I'm sorry," he said, and she knew he must have seen something that had flashed in her eyes.

"There's no need." She looked away, though, and saw a tent with his name, along with others. "Your tapes?"

"Aye."

"Doing well?"

"I had a real run after my set. But now I have an hour before the Opening Ceremonies, and I want tae buy you a drink and a meat pie." He grinned lasciviously. "I was distracted this morning, and didna ha' time tae eat."

He didn't give her a chance to respond, but practically pulled her over to a tent on the edge of a crowd. There was, apparently, a private bar there, and she requested a soft drink while he took a Bloody Mary. He spoke to someone who used a walkie-talkie and then guided her to a picnic table in back.

He leaned over and kissed her. It was swift and quite efficient, but nonetheless sexy. Very, very sexy. She felt the brush of his breath against her skin, and couldn't help but respond.

"Ah, lass, it's not fair what you do tae me."

What *she* did to *him*! If only he knew. She was like pudding inside.

But then reality came pushing in again. Robin was around somewhere. Thousands of people were around.

The pervading sound of bagpipes blared nearby, and she moved away from him, her eyes seeking the sound, and she saw not one but several groups, each dressed in different plaids, marching just feet away from them, their eyes glinting with something like approval and envy.

One bagpipe suddenly squeaked.

A chuckle started deep in Connor's throat. His mouth twitched. The skin around his eyes crinkled. "I think we may be inspiring a new tune."

Leslie heard herself giggling. She hadn't giggled in years, but she couldn't stop it. When she could finally speak, Leslie quipped, "I think the muse would prefer we wouldn't."

"Ah, you have a lovely laugh."

"You make me laugh. And smile."

His hand touched her cheek. "Don't ever stop, Leslie."

She nodded. She would have promised him the moon, and this was much less.

He took her hand and drew her down to the picnic bench. He had already placed their drinks on the table, and his gaze was turned toward the path winding around the little tent. It was as if he really did have second sight, for now a man appeared, bearing a box that he presented to Connor, who thanked him warmly.

"Have you ever had a Scottish pastry?"

She shook her head. "Not the kind you mean," she said teasingly.

"Hmmmm, now don't be putting suggestions in my head," he scolded. "I must perform, ye know, and it won't do at all if my kilt's all askew."

Leslie eyed the general area. "I think I like it that way." She had no idea what was prompting her to be so ribald and bawdy. She couldn't ever remember being like this before, but her words were just popping out.

"And you'll stand there and enjoy my . . . predicament."

She nodded.

He shook his head in mock despair. "You're a hard one."

But she wasn't, and that was the problem, she thought. All she had to do was look at him, and she melted inside; when he touched her she had no will at all.

He handed her a meat pie, which was still hot and crispy. She bit into it, relishing its spicy and delicious flavor, and her tongue darted out to lick juice from her lips.

Connor let his own pie sit while he watched, his hunger forgotten as he savored her unbridled enjoyment. He loved her when she was like this, when she allowed herself to just feel and enjoy. Her eyes glinted in the sun filtering through the trees, and its rays caught the gold in her hair. She looked up at him, her face so alive and expressive, and he remembered the first time he'd met her, how composed it had been.

It was frightening how much he wanted to tear down the barriers in her, make it impossible for her to ever repair them. He wanted to touch her, to run his fingers through that marvelous hair as he had done last night. He wanted her close to him.

He felt himself hardening again, swelling, and he swore softly to himself. This was definitely not the time. He moved away and grabbed the pie, hoping that eating might relieve some of the tension now building in him.

Leslie seemed totally oblivious to his discomfort. She was licking the last crumbs of the meat pie, and that act in itself was sensuous. But then everything about her was now sensuous to him: The way she looked at him, the way she sat, the movement of the long, slender fingers.

"Ummmm, good," she said, licking her lips once more.

"Ummmm, very good," he agreed as he leaned over and kissed those lips.

"The meat pie, I mean," she said when he released them. Considering his physical reaction minutes earlier, she tried to be circumspect, but it wasn't easy. Not when he was so close.

"That's not what *I* meant," he said, drawing near again.

She scooted away. "Remember, you warned me."

"Aye," he said wistfully. "So I did." He took a quick sip of his Bloody Mary, then another.

She had tipped her head slightly, watching him with such interest that he almost spilled the rest of the drink.

Connor tried to think of Annie and Douglas, of why he had avoided any kind of commitment since their deaths. But the reasons no longer seemed valid, not when he looked at Leslie and felt joy again, and pleasure.

For the first time in a very long while, he considered his life as it was. After the first bitter agony of his loss, he had tried to bury himself in his work. He'd prolonged his tours, sought more engagements in Scotland, and had started writing songs himself. He'd always been outgoing and had a number of friends, always had someone to go drinking with when the loneliness struck him, and he'd convinced himself that he was content.

But now he knew he'd been willing himself to forget the comfort of sharing a bed with someone he loved, of hearing a child's laughter, of being part of life rather than patching bandages on a wound that had festered. He realized he had been using his career as a defense against caring again, because not caring meant not having such intense pain.

He remembered how he felt when he woke this morning, feeling Leslie next to him, watching her wake with a drowsy sexual afterglow, and the intense satisfaction that had brought him. He hadn't realized how hollow he had been until now. He had also found himself looking forward to seeing Robin again, to hearing her quick laughter and youthful curiosity.

But the complications were enormous.

He looked down at Leslie's face, the stubborn chin, the lips that could smile so wistfully, the wide green eyes that regarded him so solemnly at times, but now impishly. He wanted to share Scotland with her, the mountains and the lakes and the wild shores. He wanted to wake up with her again and again. It was frightening how much he wanted that. But she had a life of her own here, a life and a business he knew she took pride in.

The sound of bagpipes grew louder. "Opening ceremonies," he said. "I think my presence is required."

Leslie didn't want to let him go, to share him again. She wanted to stay here in the afternoon sun, with brightly colored leaves providing a canopy as he laughed down at her. She swallowed the

need to ask him to stay. "What are you going to
sing?"

"'Scots Wha Hae,'" he said. "It comes close tae
being a national anthem." He grabbed her hand.
"Come with me."

Leslie shook her head. "I'll find Robin."

"Please. Improves my image . . . being with
the prettiest lass on the field. Unless you're worried about Robin."

Leslie felt a new surge of pleasure at his words,
at the compliment. "I would like that, and I think
Robin will fare very well on her own. Mothers are
a nuisance when you're seventeen."

"You seem more like her friend."

"I hope I'm both. I've always felt . . . that she's
missed so much."

"I think she's very lucky," he said. "And so am I."

But before she could answer, he was leading her
at a fast walk down the path, weaving in between
bagpipe groups. They finally reached the dignitary
stand, where he quickly introduced her and found
her a seat.

Several very short speeches followed, and then
Connor's turn came. The voices stilled, and she
heard the first plaintive notes of the guitar, followed by the now-familiar, now-beloved baritone
voice, strong and husky with emotion. Closing her
eyes, she pictured herself on a battlefield seven
hundred years earlier, watching the warrior Scots
defeat the larger English force. She was there, and
she felt the triumph, just as she knew everyone in
the audience was feeling it, and she realized again
how very good Connor was at what he did. He
didn't just sing; the magic of his voice took thousands of people back in time, to places across the
ocean.

She felt the love inside her swell as she heard
the feeling and heart in his voice. She was beginning to learn how great both were.

There was a moment's hush when he finished, and then the audience exploded into applause. The bagpipes started to play, and Connor joined her again, taking her hand and holding it tight as if he'd missed her for even those few brief moments.

"I've never felt like a Scot before," she whispered. "You make my one eighth feel very proud."

He leaned over. "What about your other seven eighths?"

"They're very proud too." She looked up at him and knew her face must reflect everything she felt, for he gave her the sweetest, most wonderful smile she had ever seen on a human being. There had always been electricity between them right from the beginning, but now there was something else, a bond of shared emotions, an understanding so intimate that Leslie was staggered by it. When she tried to stand, her legs were rubbery, and he reached out to steady her, transferring his considerable strength to her. The energy between them was so alive and vibrant, she knew everyone around must feel it.

The bands were marching off the field, and many in the audience were leaving the parade fields for other activities. Leslie tried to gather her wits as several people stopped to talk to her. She remembered some of them from the last two evenings, the Tattoo and the reception, but neither time had her mind worked in its usual efficient fashion, and she found herself speaking inanities.

Connor MacLaren had befuddled her mind completely. Not only her mind, she knew, but her heart as well. Dear Lord, how he had befuddled that.

Ten

The sense of magic firmly wrapped itself around Leslie through the day and into the evening.

She resolutely wiped away any nagging doubts. For the first time in many, many years, she dismissed the future. Like Scarlett O'Hara, she would think about that tomorrow.

Today . . . tonight . . . she would enjoy and keep for her mental memory book. Wonderful memories. Not bitter ones. Perhaps, she thought, it was best that all would end tomorrow, for then there could be none of the latter. She had too many of those already.

Robin and Denise joined her for Connor's set in the afternoon, and even the difficult-to-impress Denise was charmed.

Leslie had not seen him interact directly with an audience before, and he had its members eating out of his hand within a few moments. He carried on a continual patter even when he wasn't singing, joking as if each person were a friend, asking for requests, and occasionally groaning at one or another.

He sang a song called "The Gypsy Rover" for "two young friends in the audience," and winked

at Robin and Denise as they flushed with pleasure.

As he concluded "These are My Mountains," the
song he'd sung to Leslie and Robin the first night,
Leslie felt the bond between the rapt listeners and
the performer. The stage, she recognized, was his
natural element, and she realized he would never
be happy away from it. She reminded herself
again that there was no future after tonight. He
belonged to these people, to the people wherever
he went. Not to her.

*Don't let it hurt. Ignore that sick, lost feeling in
the pit of your stomach. Live for today as he does.*
When had she stopped doing that? When had she
constructed a wall against life?

When he'd completed the set, Connor moved
quickly to where Leslie stood with Robin and
Denise. "I have tae stay awhile," he said, "but I'll
pick you and Robin up at eight." He winked at
Robin and then Denise, and turned all his attention to a group of people waiting to talk with him.

Leslie finally pried herself and her two young
charges away and drove home, barely hearing
their chatter about one of the young athletes they
had met. Leslie was thinking ahead, about a hot
soak in a fragrant bath, and getting ready for
tonight. She felt like a sixteen-year-old going to
her first prom.

As Leslie slowly donned the dress he'd bought
for her, she continued to feel that certain magic,
as if she were Cinderella. She knew her daughter
felt much the same, although Robin tried to hide it
behind teenage skepticism.

Robin had been high on excitement since they'd
arrived home after dropping Denise off earlier.
She talked of a certain "Hugh" she'd met on the
festival grounds. Hugh, it seemed, lived in Jack-
sonville, Florida, and was going to be at the dance.
And Robin talked about Connor.

"He's sure knocked out about you, Mom," she said.

Leslie shook her head. "He's just a client," she cautioned.

Robin raised an eyebrow. "He doesn't look at you as if he were just a client."

Leslie wondered how he did look at her. She'd had too much of a glaze over her own eyes for the past several days to know. She tried to shrug. "He leaves tomorrow."

"He's not married, huh?"

Leslie shook her head. "His wife and son were killed in an accident years ago."

A wary look darted over Robin's face, but it was gone so swiftly, Leslie wondered if she imagined it. Her daughter shrugged, and Leslie turned her mind elsewhere, brushing her hair until it shone.

Robin was her usual self when she presented herself for inspection. Her long dark hair hung straight down her back, and in her simple dress with its plaid slung across the shoulder, she looked as if she'd walked out of a picture book.

"You're beautiful," Leslie told her daughter, thinking how grown up Robin looked, once out of the T-shirt and jeans. Another year and she would be at college. It seemed impossible. A sense of loneliness suddenly punctured Leslie's pleasure.

"You look pretty awesome yourself," Robin said, a blush spreading over her face.

Leslie shook off her foreboding. She had resolved to enjoy this night, not to let anything ruin it, not thoughts of tomorrow or next week or next year.

And it wasn't difficult to do when she opened the door to Connor. He was magnificent and elegant in a kilt and doublet, which looked like a short tuxedo jacket. He wore it over a white waistcoat and black tie, and his leather sporran had been replaced with one of fur and silver. A jeweled dagger had supplanted the plain hunting one in the kilt hose. He was, as Robin would say, awesome. And now his gaze was concentrated on Leslie as he picked up the conversation. "And I'm the luckiest man attending the ball tonight with tae of the bonniest women in Atlanta."

Robin grinned. "I can't wait to tell all my friends I went to a dance with a man in a skirt."

"Ah, now you go tae far when you make fun of the noblest of all wear," Connor retorted with mock horror.

Robin considered his kilt as thoroughly as if she were doing scientific research. "Depends on the legs. I've been doing a study today."

Connor raised his brows. "And might I ask the results?"

"Denny and I sort of put everyone on a scale of one to ten."

He chuckled. "I donna think I want tae know more," he said. "It sounds like female harassment tae me."

Robin giggled. "You sure you don't want to know where you rank?"

"I think I'll go happily through the rest of my life withou' that wee piece of knowledge," he replied.

"Coward," Robin charged.

"I think it's time to go," Leslie said. Watching as laughter floated between Connor and her daughter, she felt herself grinning at their nonsense.

She knew exactly how *she* would rank Connor, and she knew her already-flushed cheeks had probably reddened even more at the thought.

The Tartan Ball was like the rest of the festival. There was a pageantry about it that provoked more than the usual festivity that surrounded a dance.

Many women were dressed like Leslie and Robin, in long white or pastel-colored dresses with a plaid sash. Others wore long plaid skirts. With the proliferation of so many different plaids, the room was full of color.

Connor fetched them both beverages, a soft drink for Robin and glass of wine for Leslie, and both she and Robin watched with fascination as he explained what seemed very complicated movements and steps of a Scottish country dance.

The band swept into a waltz, and Connor claimed Leslie's hand, drawing her close to him. Her momentary reluctance was swept away as he so easily guided her, and her body relaxed in perfect trust. They were whirling, his strength and confidence so strong that she closed her eyes and surrendered to the pure delight of being in his arms. She had danced before, of course, but never like this. She felt as if she had been carried off by some Scottish brigand into another century, and she was spinning, spinning, in some immensely pleasurable sphere that had no beginning and no end. Leslie was filled with the sheer delight of dancing, of the sensuality of their bodies moving in such complete harmony, of pure longing as she opened her eyes and saw Connor's electric blue ones devour her with a want that echoed her own.

How could one feel such complete and pure pleasure and not explode from it?

He smiled down at her. "Happy?"

"I feel like I'm in a fairy tale. Or a movie."

He chuckled. "I get that feeling quite often at Scottish festivals."

"Living fantasies?"

He looked down at her, his eyes clouding. "It's the way I make my living, love."

"And the movie never ends?" There was another meaning in her words, and he knew it.

"It doesn't have tae."

"Doesn't it?" she asked, feeling just a bit of the foreboding she'd pushed away earlier.

"No. This movie can be the never-ending tale."

"There isn't such a thing."

"Disbeliever," he scoffed.

"I don't want to be," Leslie heard herself saying.

"Then don't be. Not taenight."

He pulled her closer to him, until she was clasped against his chest, and she heard his heart pound and smelled the intoxicatingly masculine scent he wore. She was dancing as she'd never danced before, her feet so light, she felt as if the slightest breeze could pick her up and carry her off. "You must be a sorcerer," she whispered.

Connor's lips twisted into a half-smile. There was more than a hint of sadness in it. "Then I would never allow the night tae end."

But it will, she tried to warn herself. It will. The warning didn't take, though. She was too involved with him now, with his nearness, with his magnetism. Her left foot suddenly faltered, and his strong clasp steadied her, just as it had several times earlier. She looked up at him, their gazes locking on each other as silent words passed between them, an intense desire, and something else too. A wonderful sense of belonging. She felt strangely as if they were pieces of a puzzle just fitted together, and now some nameless, impersonal being would take those pieces and rip them apart again.

The music came to a stop, and they found themselves staring at each other in the middle of the dance floor. He smiled down at her. "You're very graceful."

"Only with you," she said, for the first time revealing a part of her she hadn't dared reveal before, putting into words her own enchantment with him. But tonight she would dare anything.

"I'm glad," he replied, but his eyes said much more as he led her to where Robin stood talking to a tall, well-built young man.

His name was Hugh Carmichael, and Leslie quickly realized he was the young athlete Robin and Denise had discussed. He was built a little like a log himself, Leslie thought with some amusement as she watched Robin's slightly bedazzled eyes. Scots must be a weakness in her family, she thought as Hugh led her daughter onto the floor and directed her through a Scottish dance, both of them laughing at her missteps.

"Would you like tae try?" Connor asked.

Leslie shook her head. If she thought she could concentrate, she supposed she would love it. She had always liked dancing, but now . . .

The same thought had obviously run through his mind. "Guid," Connor said. "Let's go." He grabbed her hand and led the way out the door. The dance was at the same hotel where he was staying, and he deftly guided her through a crowded foyer and lobby, and toward the elevators.

She couldn't think. The skin where his hand touched was like fire. She shivered, but how can you shiver when all you feel is heat? Now-familiar sensations were roiling around inside her. The very fierceness of them made her catch her breath as she hurried her steps to keep up with his.

Leslie was oblivious now to anything but Connor, ignoring whether Robin would note her absence, or whether anyone was watching them practically gallop toward the elevator. She cared only about the vital, handsome man next to her, the man who would leave tomorrow.

Her hand clenched his tightly.

There were, she soon discovered, several advantages in Scottish wear. She'd already discovered the kilt's assets. Now, as Connor's fingers deftly unbuttoned the back of her dress, she found another advantage. As he peeled the long garment away, his hands slid down the length of her body. She wore only a bra and panties underneath, not much more than he, and then they were standing together, his skin touching and branding hers before he lifted her easily and carried her to the bed.

"I wanted tae do this all day," he said as his mouth kissed the side of her neck, moving slowly upward, nuzzling, arousing.

Last night had been searching, discovering. Tonight was explosive. Explosive and desperate.

Leslie knew they were both grabbing, trying to consume the last contents of the barrel like two starving people. Her body had instinctively arched toward his in an agony of need, and after the slightest pause to don protection, he came into her hard and fast.

Then the gentleness of last night returned, that slow, seductive rhythm as his mouth reached for hers. With every subtle movement he loved her, firing the coil of warmth until it became a roaring blaze. She matched him stroke for stroke, acting as she had on the dance floor, with complete understanding and trust and harmony. The frantic need slowed into something giving, into prolonging the exquisiteness of being a part of each other, until the world seemed to shatter in an explosion of rapture.

Leslie could barely breathe when the last shudder had passed, the last tremor slaking in an aftermath of incredible sweetness. They lay next to each other, their hands still clinging together.

"Leslie," he breathed hoarsely. "Dear God in heaven."

Leslie couldn't say anything at all. She'd never

felt such a complexity of overwhelming emotions. She was physically sated, but her mind felt ready to explode with the implications of what had just happened—her complete lack of control, the fire that still glowed within her for him. It would always glow for him.

"We'd better go back," she said hesitantly. "Robin . . ."

"Robin looked well occupied. . . ."

"But what will she think?"

"What do *you* think?" His voice was suddenly very intense.

She didn't ask about what. She knew. He'd said last night he didn't want things to end between them. But what kind of future could they have? She knew from previous experience that absence did not make the heart fonder. At least long, frequent absences. A sharp break now would be more merciful than a long, lingering death.

But she pretended an ignorance. "About what?"

His gaze pierced her, as if he knew she was stalling. "Ah, Leslie, love. You know there's something . . . very strong between us. Are you willing tae give it a chance?"

"It's impossible," she said.

"Nothing is impossible. I can come back tae Atlanta several times before I return tae Scotland, and then you and Robin can come over."

"No." The word was sharper than she intended, almost like a dagger thrust. In her own heart, as well as his.

"Why?"

"Because it wouldn't work."

"Why?"

"Because I've been through it before," she whispered in self-defense at his probing.

His hand, which had been running softly up and down her arm, stopped. "Through what before?"

"I told you my husband was a musician," Leslie said.

There was a long silence. "You said he died of an overdose?"

"Six years after he left me . . . which he did as soon as he discovered I was pregnant. But he'd really left long before that—when he started touring. There were . . . women, drugs, alcohol." Leslie hated the pain and uncertainty in her voice.

"And you think I'm like tha'?" The accent was thick again, as she'd learned it usually became when he felt something deeply. Now, it was anger, plain and clear.

"No," she said, realizing that she meant it. "But . . . I don't think I can ever go through that again, the waiting, the uncertainty of when, or even if, he was coming back." She heard her voice quiver slightly.

"You *are* saying you believe I'm like tha'." His voice was very quiet.

Leslie winced at the bitter accusation she heard there.

"We ha' better go back down," he said, getting to his feet in one fluid movement. His voice was impersonal, too impersonal.

Leslie shivered, as if a cold wind had swept through the room, chasing all the warmth away. She felt as if she'd suddenly lost something very important, and she didn't know how to get it back. She had hurt him—badly, from the tight set of his mouth—and she couldn't take back the implications she had made. Perhaps because they were still so embedded inside her. Damn Tommy.

But she couldn't blame everything on him. She should have let go long before this. If there was anything she knew, deep inside herself, it was that Connor MacLaren was nothing at all like Tommy Turner. But even so, there were insurmountable problems between them. Connor lived in Scotland, and she here, and she didn't think she could ever surrender her independence again, not even for Connor MacLaren. It had been too difficult to obtain. And without it, a woman became so vulnerable.

Even if her heart melted every time she looked at him, she couldn't make another mistake . . . not for her daughter's sake, not for her own.

But she couldn't take her eyes away from him as he dressed. And when his gaze settled back on her, he seemed to have thawed slightly. He reached out his hand to her, and she took it, allowing him to pull her closely to him.

"I love you, Leslie. I didna really think I would ever love anyone again after Annie, and God knows I didna think it could happen in a week, but now I'm not ready tae throw it awa'."

She allowed him to enclose her in his arms for one unforgettable moment. She allowed all her feelings free rein. After that momentary coldness his embrace was warm and solid and understanding.

And oh so wonderful.

Robin was dancing again when they found their way back to the ballroom.

Connor had said no more about the future, but had merely helped her dress and watched as she repaired her lipstick. Leslie felt his invisible restraint and recognized the tension within him. There was similar tension in her.

There was no outward evidence of it, however, as he drew her on the floor during one of the few slow numbers. All the earlier magic of his body radiated through her, and she knew the loss of it would create a permanent coldness. And yet . . .

The evening sped by. The last evening. The last time she would see him. Leslie knew he planned to leave tomorrow evening, and that would be the end of her own special fairy tale. She had made that clear to him. At least she thought she had.

She was barely aware when Hugh Carmichael asked her to dance. He was not nearly as adept a dancer as Connor, and she had to pay attention. Yet she could see Connor dancing with Robin, see her laughing up at him. He had seemed to bring them both alive, she and Robin. Was there possibly a way . . . ?

The more she thought of it, the more hopeless it appeared. He had never said anything about marriage, and even if he had, she didn't think she could uproot Robin and herself, and all the security she had so carefully woven around the two of them.

"I would like to call on Robin, if you wouldn't object," Hugh was saying.

The words finally penetrated. "I thought you lived in Florida."

"I do, but I have friends here. I also play the bagpipes and sometimes come up to play with some bands."

Leslie decided she liked him, liked him very much indeed. She didn't know young men asked parents' permission anymore. Certainly none of Robin's other dates, rare as they were, did. Not a bad custom at all. "Of course I wouldn't," she said, and watched as he beamed.

She wondered if she had beamed like that earlier.

Connor reclaimed her and guided her through a Scottish dance, and then they were speaking to people he knew. Much too soon, people started leaving, and the band played "Auld Lang Syne." Leslie had always felt the song one of the saddest, most wistful songs in the world, and now it seemed even more so. It always signified separation, leave-takings, and she'd never associated it with happy times.

She felt Connor's hand go around her shoulder, and the room reverberated with voices singing along as she felt the world dropping away from her.

The evening had been like a fairy tale, except for those few last moments in his hotel room, the moments when reality had crashed upon her. That same reality was intruding again, and she realized everything was over.

Robin chattered most of the way home, about Hugh mostly. She was ready to take highland dancing lessons, maybe even learn to play the bagpipe. This from a girl who five days ago disdained anything with a low decibel level. Of course, Leslie had recently discovered that a badly played bagpipe could produce a sound that made heavy metal sound good even to her.

When they arrived at the house, Robin thanked Connor, giving him an old-world curtsy that even further shocked Leslie, and walked demurely inside.

Leslie was about to do the same, quickly, before he could see tears gathering at the corner of her eyes, but he grabbed her hand and imprisoned her next to him.

"No' so fast," Connor said, and his lips came down on hers, hard and possessive and commanding.

Leslie tried to hold herself apart from him, but she couldn't. Her lips melted into his, her quiet desperation transforming into raw, ragged need.

There was nothing tender about him. The kiss was demanding, and she knew he was trying to impose his will upon her, that he was telling her he wasn't going to let go.

Perhaps not tonight . . .

But the tomorrows were limited.

With the small cry of a wounded animal, she tore herself away and jerked open the car door, and ran up the steps. She heard a door slam behind her and other rushing footsteps, and then he had her in his arms.

"Don't throw this away."

"You live in Scotland. . . ."

"We'll work it out."

"I have a business. Robin loves it here."

"I love you, Leslie."

"Love . . . is for the young."

"I donna think you really believe that."

"It's not love," she cried out. "It's just . . ."

His hands had captured her shoulders and when she looked up at him, he was glaring down at her. "Lust?" he said. "I sincerely hope so. But it's much more, and you know it."

He kissed her again, this time the anger melding into something tender, and her body glided into all his now-familiar hard curves, seeking their comfort and warmth. "I willna go until you say you'll see me taemorrow."

"You're leaving."

"I'll leave Monday. I don't have a performance until that night."

"It will just make it worse."

"It canna get any worse, Leslie." She wished her name didn't sound like a song on his lips. "Or better," he added.

She thought of Robin inside. In the porch light she and Connor were only too visible. But she didn't want to leave. That was the hell of things. He dulled her will, sedated her conviction.

And made her senses so alive.

"Say you'll see me."

"Yes," she agreed in a daze.

He grinned then, the wonderful grin that could charm the world. "I'll come by after the last performance tomorrow."

Leslie could only nod her head, for once eclipsed by a will greater than her own.

Eleven

Robin was standing awkwardly near the stairs when Leslie pushed back a lock of hair that had fallen on her forehead and tried to straighten her expression. The brightness had faded from her daughter's eyes. An anxious expression had taken its place, even a bit of shock, and Leslie knew her daughter had seen that last desperate kiss.

"Mom?"

"What, love?"

"You aren't thinking . . . about doing anything . . . drastic?"

There was so much uncertainty in her daughter's voice that Leslie's heart dropped.

"Drastic?"

"Like . . . fall in love?"

That's exactly what she had done. Leslie swallowed, stalling for time. She'd tried never to lie to her daughter. Lies caused too much hurt and created breaches that could never be mended. If you didn't have trust, you didn't have anything. Yet Robin looked very young and vulnerable, a kind of fear in her face.

"I'm not sure, Robin. I think so."

"How could you?" The fear was greater now.

"I thought you liked him."

"As your friend . . . like the others. Not . . ." Robin's voice dropped off, and her lips trembled. "It's always been the two of us."

And you will be off to college next year, and I'll be alone. Leslie felt the chill she'd felt earlier in Connor's room. She'd made Robin her life for so many years, had woven a cocoon around herself and her daughter that no one could pierce. She had done it to protect Robin; at least, she had told herself that, but had she accomplished her goal too well, made each too dependent on the other?

"You'd disapprove of more?" she asked now.

"You're my mother. You always said I was enough for you."

Leslie heard the insecurity in Robin's voice, and the jealousy, the same jealousy she'd felt for the crowds that surrounded Connor.

"I love you, Robin. Nothing will ever change that."

"I don't want *anything* to change."

Leslie felt sick. For a few fleeting moments tonight she'd thought, hoped, perhaps a miracle could happen. But all such thoughts came crashing down in flames. Robin looked so young and lost at the moment, so unlike the vibrant girl earlier this evening.

She owed her daughter. Robin had never had a father, never had so many things.

"He's leaving Monday," Leslie said in the calmest voice she could.

"I thought he was leaving tomorrow." There was a thread of suspicion in Robin's voice.

"He doesn't finish until late tomorrow, so he decided to wait until Monday morning."

"Are you going back to the festival tomorrow?"

Leslie hadn't known until that very moment. She wanted to—oh how she wanted to! But that would only make things worse. He dug deeper into her heart every time she saw him, heard him, spent time with him. He'd already completely negated her ability to say no.

"I don't think so," she said finally, carefully watching Robin's face. There was a certain amount of relief on it—relief and guilt.

Leslie ached inside for herself and for Robin. Everything had happened too fast. She felt her life was spiraling out of control, like a top. How could she give up a single splendid, giddy, wondrous moment with Connor MacLaren? Yet she had no right. Robin had no one but her.

She went over to her daughter and hugged her. "You're the most important person to me, Robin. Don't ever think otherwise." She tried to keep her voice light. "Now, let's have some cocoa, and you can tell me all about Hugh. He asked me if I would mind if he dated you."

As she heated some milk, Leslie only half listened to Robin's relieved voice. She felt like a zombie, barely alive. But then, she had been like this for years. She just hadn't realized it until Connor had stirred her from her half-somnolent state. She hadn't known she could feel so incredibly alive, so . . . She bit her lip as she felt the burning inside her again, the remembrance of how he felt and tasted and . . .

"You're not listening."

Robin's accusing voice penetrated. "Of course I am," Leslie defended herself. "Why don't we go and have brunch someplace tomorrow?" Anything to stop thinking.

"I can't," Robin replied, a little sheepishly. "I told Hugh I would come watch him tomorrow. He's competing again."

Leslie very carefully poured the cocoa into two cups. Silently she nodded and picked up her mug.

"He's really nice, Mom," Robin said. "I think he's a little worried because I'm still in high school."

Leslie had suspected as much, and thought that was why he had asked her for her permission. Yet Robin would be off to college next year and would be with young men then. In some ways Robin was very mature for her age, more so than most of the high school boys Leslie had met, which is why she suspected Robin didn't date much. But Leslie realized that, as mature as Robin sometimes acted, she was still a child in many ways. Her momentary insecurity a few minutes earlier showed that only too well. She had been Leslie's little girl again, afraid of the dark, of the unknown.

Perhaps she, Leslie, was afraid too.

She sat and listened, her eyes focused on Robin but not really seeing her. She was seeing herself at Robin's age, ready to hurl herself into life. Connor had brought that girl back, had made her eager to adventure and explore. Could she ever go back again to her nice, safe cave?

Robin was looking at her strangely, and Leslie finished the cocoa. "I think it's time to go to bed," she said.

"Mom," Robin said slowly as though she sensed some of her mother's feelings. "I thought you were happy."

"I thought so too, love," Leslie replied a bit wistfully. She rose and placed her cup in the sink, stopped to lean over and lightly kiss Robin on the cheek. "Good night."

"Sleep tight, and don't let the bedbugs bite," Robin replied with a small smile. It had been a long time since she had recited that bedtime ritual.

Leslie smiled back, remembering, and then left her daughter sitting at the table.

Leslie knew he would come the next afternoon. She'd thought about leaving the house, manufacturing an errand, but she wasn't going to run away. She'd already done too much of that through the years.

Robin had come home for a short while, reporting that Hugh had won third place in one of the contests and had started back to Florida. She didn't mention Connor. After a few awkward minutes she said she was going to run over to Denise's for a while.

Leslie went back to cleaning the house. It was uncharacteristically spotless already. She had tried to work on an upcoming project for her developer client, but her mind didn't function. So she had started cleaning the house. She'd scrubbed the kitchen and bathroom floors, vacuumed the rugs, scrubbed the floors again. They'd never been so clean.

She thought about changing clothes. She had put on an old, oversize sweatshirt and pair of jeans, but that act—changing clothes—would be cheating, a traitorous act to what she must do. She didn't know why exactly, but something told her it would be. As if she were trying to impress him when really all she could do was to tell him good-bye. Thank you and good-bye.

He had given her an invaluable gift, the gift of those bright, shining moments that she would never forget, that she would always treasure. And then they both could get on with their own individual lives.

Individual. What a lonely sound, all of a sudden.

When she heard the car turn into the driveway, she stood stock-still, unable to move. How could someone feel such contradictory things at one time: Unbearable sadness, spontaneous happiness? They batted back and forth like a tennis ball.

When she finally forced herself to open the door, the happiness assumed dominance. Connor had changed into dark slacks and a dark blue seaman's sweater.

There was no smile on his face, which looked unusually solemn as he gazed down at her. Leslie suddenly wished she had changed her clothes after all; she felt like a child in her oversize shirt and baggy jeans and no makeup.

"You aren't going tae ask me in?"

Leslie felt rooted to the floor, but she finally forced herself to move. She wished he didn't have such a powerful effect on her, that he didn't reduce her to idiocy every time she saw him.

"I wasn't sure . . . didn't know . . ." She faltered.

"Whether I would come? Ah, Leslie, I told you I would. When will you start having faith?"

"I don't know," she said wretchedly. And she didn't. Not the kind of faith that convinced her everything would, could, work out.

"We'll work on that, love," he said. "I missed you today."

"I had work to do. I've . . . been neglecting it."

"Robin was there."

"Did you talk to her?" The words were almost breathless.

He shook his head. "I saw her briefly, but I think she's also running away from me. I dinna know I was such an ogre." There was a very definite question in his voice.

"She saw us last night. I think it frightened her a little."

"Changes are always a wee bit frightening. But without change there's no growth. I'm learning that myself. And it's no' so easy."

Connor. Who always seemed so sure of himself. Leslie found his words difficult to believe, and it must have showed on her face, for he leaned down and kissed her lightly. "I'm probably just as terrified as Robin."

They were both still standing in the hallway, staring at each other, unable to let go, gaze for gaze. "Why?" Leslie finally managed.

He took her hand, and together they went into the living room and sat on the couch. He pulled her in his arms, leaning her back against his chest.

"I told you I was married, and my son and wife were killed in an accident. I was on tour at the time. Douglas wanted tae come wi' me, but there was school and . . . Annie never really liked the road."

Leslie heard the slow sigh that came, the uncharacteristically labored telling that reflected pain, and she hurt for him. She hurt more for him than she ever had for herself. She waited for him to continue, although part of her didn't want to hear what she feared was coming.

"Annie was taking our son tae a birthday party. She didn't like tae drive, and I always drove when I was home. But I wasn't there." He hesitated before continuing in a harsh tone, "She lost control in a rainstorm and ran into another car. Both she and my son were killed." His hands tightened around Leslie's. "She was never very guid at driving. I should have been there." It was a cry of pain, of frustration, of guilt.

Leslie understood guilt. She understood loss, although not the kind she knew he'd experienced. She had never lost a child. She couldn't imagine losing Robin, or the agony of feeling she might have somehow prevented the loss.

Her hand brought his to her mouth, and she pressed it against her lips, wanting to share his pain and take some of the burden on herself.

"I've always avoided relationships since then," he added slowly. "Until you." He didn't add that he feared he could never accept the risks again.

"Tell me about her," Leslie said. She sensed his

need to talk, and she wanted to know more, wanted to know all there was to know about him. And the woman he'd loved.

"She was gentle and lovely, with long auburn hair. She loved being a mother. She was very guid at it. Like you are. Her name was Annie, and I called her Annie Laurie. It was . . . a special song for us."

Leslie's breath caught in her throat. She remembered when she had asked him to sing that song, and he'd refused. The pain in his voice was still raw, and she thought he must have loved his wife a great deal to feel so deeply after so long a time. How could she ever compete with those kinds of memories?

The fingers of his left hand absently ruffled her hair, and Leslie felt an uncertainty in him that was rare. The air between them was charged, full of voltaic energy. So many unsaid words, thoughts, hung in the air; saying them required decisions neither was ready to make, so they allowed them to drift like storm clouds above.

But the nearness of one to the other prompted a decision they could make. Not only could, but must. Like a piece of iron to a lodestone.

He leaned down and kissed her.

It was unlike the others, almost cruel, as if he were trying to banish something. Or prove something.

But the lack of tenderness found response in Leslie. There was a violence in the exchange, a primitive need so strong, it overwhelmed her. Overwhelmed and excited. Overwhelmed and taunted. Overwhelmed and . . . set ablaze every feeling part of her.

She was barely able to think, to comprehend the whisper in the back of her brain. When his lips moved, the whisper in her mind formed the word "Robin."

Connor groaned.

Leslie felt his arousal, and the core of her felt the same frustration she knew he must be feeling. She hurt, agonized, ached.

"Will you come back tae the hotel with me?"

Leslie knew she shouldn't. She was in so deep already. Her heart, her body, her senses. They were already swamped by the pure animal vitality of him, the magnetism of his eyes, the sensuality of his touch.

She nodded.

They drove in silence. Leslie was stunned by her lack of willpower, by the effect he had on her. She had sworn no one would ever have that kind of power over her again.

But then, no one had been able to turn her inside out as Connor MacLaren did.

And during those moments he'd talked about his family, she'd felt more connected to him than to any man she'd ever known. She'd felt his grief and shared it. She'd watched him laugh and knew his joy, and she'd heard him sing his love for his homeland. She'd seen so many parts of him in such a short time, and she liked every one of them.

Yet everyone hid parts of themselves. She knew from some of his silences that he had dark corners, just as she had. And those dark corners prevented anything except the here and now.

But she would take that.

She was barely aware of the walk up to his room, of his subtle guidance, of the key opening the door. She was aware of little but the way her body wanted to gravitate to his.

And it did—the moment the door closed behind them.

She savored his warmth and strength as he

reached out for her, as his hands undressed her and then himself with a deft efficiency that was quite incredible. And then his body was reaching for her, and the gentleness was back—the gentleness and the caring and the loving.

And the fierceness. The wild Scots fierceness that made her heart sing with haunting, irresistible longing, then sweet, exquisite pleasure, and finally . . . an explosion of rapture and the slow, tumbling ripples of ecstasy mixed with a pain so sweet and piercing, she trembled.

She pressed her head against his chest, and wondered how he could breathe when her own breath was somehow caught in her throat.

She loved him. She loved him so much that every part of her ached from it. Her hand went up and caught a falling lock of his hair, pushing it back with a gesture that was so natural, she felt she'd been doing it for years. Every crevice of his face was familiar now—familiar and loved and ever so dear.

"Oh, Leslie," he groaned. "Dear God, I donna want tae leave you. I canna leave you."

Yet they both knew he would. He had to. He had commitments just as she had.

"Will you . . . would you consider moving tae Scotland?" His words were tentative, as if he were trying them out for the first time.

Leslie stiffened. Of course the idea had crossed her mind, but she had instantly dismissed it. Connor had never said anything about marriage, or a long-term commitment. And they had been together only a week; she had always felt whatever it was between them would end today, that it had to end.

She shook her head slowly. "There's Robin, and the business, and my home and—"

"I want Robin tae," he interrupted. "She would love Scotland."

Leslie shook her head. "I don't think so. She's in her senior year of high school, looking forward to college."

Connor was silent, but his hold on her tightened.

"And there's my business. It's taken Gillian and me years to build it. It's just now becoming successful."

"I . . . need publicity, a manager. . . ."

"No, you don't," she said gently. "You would have done very well without me this week. And I worked very hard for the Word Shop." She took his hand in hers, willing him to understand.

"I married Tommy when I was eighteen, just out of high school, despite my parents' objections. We hadn't known each other long—he was a friend of a friend of mine, and he was already gathering a following in Atlanta and the South. I think he married me because I was a challenge . . . probably the only girl who didn't fall into bed with him at the crook of his finger. But I was dazzled, too dazzled to see that I was nothing but a challenge, a toy he felt he was being denied and thus had to have."

Leslie felt his hand rub her arms as he had done before, a comforting, soothing movement. A possessive movement. Her gaze went up and met his.

"His interest didn't last much longer than a month. Then there was a new 'challenge,' and another. I should have left him then, but my father had been bitterly opposed to the marriage, and I couldn't admit making such a bad mistake, couldn't go crawling home. So I stayed with Tommy as he tore my confidence apart piece by piece. And then I was pregnant, and he became . . . abusive. He didn't want a child. It would ruin his image, he said.

"He was touring then, and making a lot of money, but he spent it as fast as he received it.

Women, drugs. He gave me very little money. Where does a pregnant, unskilled nineteen-year-old go?" Leslie knew some of her old bewilderment, the old desperation, was in her voice.

"I finally went home, and I'll never forget how I felt. A failure. A fool. Even worse than that. Tommy had made me feel worthless, a burden. Not long after I went home, my father died, and he didn't leave much. Mom took care of Robin while I worked during the day and went to Georgia State at night. It took six years to get my degree."

Leslie hesitated, searching his face for his reaction, then she continued, very deliberately, so he would understand. "I didn't get to spend much time with Robin, but I finally graduated. Even then, it was hard. Mom died, and all I could find was a secretarial job with a public-relations agency. It took me four years to become an account executive, and during the first recession I was laid off. I met Gillian, and we started our own firm, but it took another couple of years before the Word Shop was really established and making a good profit." She turned and looked at Connor steadily. "It's the only security I've ever had, Connor. It's my independence."

Leslie swallowed, wondering at the absence of the usual rush of pleasure and accomplishment that came when she talked about her business. There was only a hollow feeling instead.

And the silence that followed did nothing to fill it. There was only a hopelessness now, a sense of emptiness as they slowly understood the meaning of what seemed like irreconcilable differences.

Twelve

Lead seemed to weigh down Conner's stomach.

He'd recognized her commitment to her business, but he hadn't known how deep that commitment ran, or all the reasons for it.

But even as he understood them now, he also realized that, although he had asked her to come to Scotland, he hadn't asked her to marry him. He understood the reasons for that too.

And now he couldn't pursue it. Not now that he knew her own needs. How, understanding what he did now, could he bring her to Scotland and then leave her continually? Yet how else could he support her and Robin?

He buried his face in her hair, in the soft, fragrant auburn hair he'd come to cherish. "I'm going tae miss you more than you'll ever know."

"Oh I do know," she murmured.

"I'll come back."

"I don't know if that's wise," Leslie heard herself say. She knew it wasn't. This was going to be a terrible wrench. How many times could she go through it?

"I donna think I have a choice," he said.

"Once you're gone . . ." Leslie started, but he shook his head.

"No, love. I donna think it works that way. Not this." His smile was wry, even sad.

"It has to," Leslie said. "I can't live on maybes and tomorrows."

He expelled a long, deep breath. "Will you compromise? Meet me different places?"

"I can't. I have Robin."

"You have *you* tae," Connor said gently.

"Robin doesn't approve."

He stilled. "She said that?"

"She saw us kissing last night."

Connor groaned. "I was afraid of that when she seemed tae avoid me taeday."

"She's still very much a child in some ways. I'm the only parent she has—has ever had."

"And in the next few years . . . when she's an adult and wants her own independence and her own family?"

Leslie was silent. God knew she had thought of that last night. Was she giving up a lifetime for a few months of making Robin happy? But there was so much more than that. Her own sense of worth, her own security.

"Don't gi' up on us, love." He leaned over and kissed her, long and hard. "I promise I won't."

And then he entered her again, this time slowly, making love with his body, with his mouth, with every movement. He teased and stirred and then slowly brought her with him to a shattering climax.

When the last shudder had stopped, he moved next to her, holding her tightly, and they were silent. Leslie simply savored the feel of him next to her, storing up the memories, hoping it would be enough but knowing it wouldn't.

● ● ●

He said good-bye at the door.

He took her chin in his hand and kissed her lingeringly.

"Here," he said, thrusting something into her hands.

She looked at the clipped papers blindly. "What is it?"

"My schedule. If you need anything, and even if you donna . . ."

The offer was left there. Tantalizingly.

Leslie clutched the papers tightly as though they were a lifeline, even though she knew she would not use them. She couldn't.

"I'll call you," he said after a short silence.

She shook her head.

"I'll call." His voice was firm.

His lips brushed her forehead. "Good night, lass."

And then he was gone.

Connor looked out over the audience in the Nashville theater. It was full, a fact that usually gave him pleasure. But some of the relish was gone. It had been gone since he left Atlanta. He had driven here, keeping his rental car, and it had been an infernally lonely ride. From here he would go to Memphis for a performance and then up to Chicago. From there, he would fly to San Francisco.

But the hills and valleys of Tennessee had blurred today. The sun had even dulled. Mile by mile, he knew he was moving away from something that had refired the core of him, that had brought tenderness back into his life.

Mile by mile.

Until he'd met Leslie, he'd looked forward to this trip, to driving through the southeast region in fall, when it was in full color. He particularly liked

Southern audiences; they were always very receptive and enthusiastic. But now . . .

The requests from the audience came quickly. Connor felt he hadn't been at peak performance, but perhaps there was something new and fresh in his music. The spectators were certainly enthusiastic.

He liked this kind of theater, small and intimate. The stage was plain, with only a stool and a microphone. It was only him and his guitar, and both of them were interacting and conversing with members of the audience as if they were old friends.

Connor should have been happy. Content.

But every time he saw a flash of red hair, hope leapt inside him, only to die when the individual turned her head. He looked for her in every seat, even knowing she wouldn't be there.

"Sing 'Annie Laurie.'"

The request came from deep in the audience. He hesitated. He usually just shook his head and took another request quickly without explanation. But now he just breathed deeply. How could he expect Leslie to shake *her* past when he was still so affected by his own? How could he expect *her* to make changes when he wasn't willing to do the same?

It had been a very long time since he had played it, eight years to be exact, but he could never forget it. His fingers strummed the first notes, and his voice faltered on the initial words, then came strong and true.

And some of the pain started to fade. The loss would always be with him, but its sharp edge dulled with each succeeding word, and the good memories came flooding back.

> *"And like winds in summer sighing*
> *Her voice is low and sweet.*

Her voice is low and sweet,
And she's a' the world tae me.
And for bonnie Annie Laurie
I'd lay me doon and dee."

As he drew out the last sad note, he breathed
deeply, and he felt suddenly free. He heard the
applause wash over him, but that was minor
compared to the realization flooding him. "Lay me
doon and dee." He knew with sudden insight that
he had, in part, done that. And that he was ready
to live again, to put Annie and Douglas in the past,
to put his guilt there too.

He was no longer ready to "lay doon and dee."

Connor couldn't wait now for the set to end. He
had never told Leslie he loved her, had never
asked her to marry him. Although he'd invited her
to come to Scotland, to see him, he had never
really committed himself.

He was barely aware of the rest of the songs he
sang, or of the applause.

He had plans to make.

It had been three days since he'd left, and Leslie
prowled her house like a lost spirit seeking salva-
tion. She waited impatiently for Robin to come
home. She needed to get out of the house, away
from every place Connor had been. He was a
constant ghost.

What she needed was a ghostbuster.

The week had been one of the worst she had
ever spent. She'd even found herself two days
earlier buying a cassette player for the office.
She'd told herself she needed some good classical
music to cleanse her mind, and then she sat there
and listened to Connor's tapes. Even a call from
Gillian, saying she would return tomorrow, Thurs-

day, didn't help, though work was piling up. Leslie just couldn't concentrate. Not anymore.

When Robin finally arrived home from a painting lesson, Leslie suggested going out to dinner, and Robin, uncommonly quiet, agreed. They decided on a small Mexican restaurant they both liked. No ghosts there.

Robin ordered her usual tacos, but she kept looking at Leslie strangely as her mother picked at her food.

"Where did Connor go?" Robin finally asked.

Leslie stiffened. "Nashville, Memphis, I think." She didn't think at all. She knew. She knew where he was going to be every minute. She'd looked at the schedule often enough, reached for the phone often enough, jerked her hand back often enough.

"You really liked him, didn't you?"

"He was a client," Leslie said in her most matter-of-fact voice.

"You never go out with your other clients."

Leslie shrugged. "They never asked me." That was a lie, and she knew her face flushed with the evidence of it.

"Will he come back?"

Leslie shrugged. "I don't think so."

"I shouldn't have said what I did Saturday. I was . . . sort of . . . freaked out."

Leslie couldn't contain her surprise. "What brought this on?"

"You look . . . so miserable. You've looked so miserable for the past few days. And . . ."

"And?"

"I . . . was being selfish. I didn't want anything to change. But it's going to, Mother. Next year, it's going to when I go to college. I can't believe I was so . . . stupid. It was just so . . . sudden."

Leslie was silent for a moment. "It's not just you, love. It's the business too."

"I've never seen your face glow when you come home from work, not like it did when you were with him," Robin said. "You've always told me to grab at the ring. Don't you think you should practice what you preach?"

Was she that transparent? Was it that obvious? Leslie just shook her head. "There's no way it could work, Robin."

"Did you talk about trying?"

"He lives in Scotland, I live here." She had avoided answering the question well and true, and Robin knew it.

"You did, then?" Robin persisted.

Leslie shrugged. "It wouldn't work. No way. There are many reasons. And I only knew him a week."

"I don't think time matters," Robin said thoughtfully. "It's like Hugh. When I met him, I knew he was special."

Leslie sat straight in her chair. "Special?"

"Don't look that way, Mom. I'm going to college, but I do think . . ." Her voice trailed off.

"That Hugh is special," Leslie repeated for her.

"Aye," Robin said with a grin. "Do you think it's a family weakness?"

"But you're just starting your life, and I have . . ."

"I know," Robin said. "A business. But which would you rather have. Connor or a sterile office?"

Put that way, Leslie thought wryly, there wasn't much choice. When did her daughter get so wise?

She searched for another topic. She needed time to think. "Would you like to go to a movie?"

"Yeah."

"Me too, yeah," Leslie said, trying to summon some enthusiasm, surprised at Robin's assent. They hadn't gone to a movie together in a year, maybe more. There was never enough time.

Where did it go?

And did she want to spend the rest of her life wondering whether she'd made the best use of it?

It was a four-hour drive to Memphis from Nashville, and every hour took Connor farther away from what he wanted most.

Thursday. And Thursday meant Memphis. He felt thoroughly frustrated. He had called Leslie four times last night . . . until midnight, and then again this morning. No answer.

During the drive to Memphis he devised a new plan.

It wasn't going to be easy, but . . .

Connor saw Leslie slipping through his fingers, like tiny diamonds. The farther he traveled, the more convinced of it he became.

Desperation continued to spur creative thinking. He could stay in the United States part of the year. If he was married to a U.S. citizen, he would have no problems there. As soon as Robin finished high school, she could come to Scotland each summer. And Leslie's business? He knew a number of performers; perhaps she could continue either here or in Scotland. It would take adjustments, of course, but then anything worthwhile required compromise and change.

He only knew he didn't want to leave her, couldn't leave her or he might well lay "doon and dee."

Leslie picked Gilly up at the airport on Thursday. Gilly, as usual, talked a mile a minute, and it took her a while to notice how quiet Leslie was.

"How was Connor MacLaren?"

Gilly's sharp inquiry cut right through Leslie's fragile defenses.

She shrugged and wished her face didn't show every emotion she felt.

"That well, huh?"

Leslie was silent, her heart thumping even at the sound of his name. And then she realized his tape was playing in the stereo. Nothing else had played for the last three days.

"Is he as good-looking as his pictures?"

Leslie nodded wordlessly.

"For some reason I didn't get the impression he was a real Romeo."

"He's not," Leslie leapt to his defense.

"Nor a love-'em-and-leave-'em type."

The car took on a sudden burst of speed.

"How did he like Robin or, more to the point, how did Robin like him?"

"He's just a client, Gilly."

"Once more with conviction, Les," Gilly taunted her. "Is he coming back?"

"What's the use?" Leslie finally exploded. "There's no possible way . . ."

"There's always a way, my friend."

"Big talk from someone who never dates anyone twice."

"Just wait until the right man comes along," Gilly said seriously.

"Are you trying to get rid of me?"

"You know you're the only person who could put up with me," Gilly said. "I would hate to lose you, but something tells me I already have."

"Nothing's going to change."

There was a disbelieving silence from Gilly's part of the car.

"Nothing," Leslie reaffirmed.

But even she knew it had.

Leslie knew exactly how much things had changed later that day. She had forgotten an appointment with her developer. She *never* forgot appointments.

What was even worse was her lack of concern when Steven Morrow called to find out whether anything had happened to her.

No, lack of concern was not exactly the right term. She did care, because she deplored discourtesy, but in the most honest part of her soul she knew that meeting had simply ranked fairly low in a consciousness dominated by a black-haired troubadour. Still, she made very contrite apologies, blessed Steven for being understanding, arranged another meeting, and resolved not to miss it.

Still . . .

Connor had not called. She had told him not to, of course, but she hungered for that contact.

She had been foolish to believe she could go back to being what she was. She had been given a piece of heaven and offered even more, and she had been too afraid to accept.

Even Robin and Gilly knew it.

She had shut the door on him, given him no encouragement, and she was beginning to realize how self-defeating that was. She owed it to both of them to give it a chance.

And she had to tell him that. She didn't think she could do it on the phone. He would be in Chicago Friday night and Saturday, according to his schedule. She would fly up and see whether it was too late.

Please God, don't let it be too late.

She made her plane reservations for Saturday. Robin could stay with her friend Denise. They had bunked together before.

And Steve Morrow? Gilly owed her. Gilly could take over Steve Morrow. Even if they didn't particularly like each other. Even if Gilly thought him a pompous jock, and he thought Gilly eccentric. The thought made her smile for the first time in days.

The heaviness in her lifted, and her feet felt as light as they had on the dance floor just days ago.

Thirteen

"Chicago!"

Gilly had felt the force of Connor MacLaren's personality over the phone, and it still came through with immediate, physical impact.

"Yep," she said. "I think she wanted to see a certain folksinger."

Connor felt his frustration replaced by a slowly spreading river of pleasure. He had spent all day, all week, in fact, trying unsuccessfully to reach Leslie, and had decided to fly to Atlanta Sunday. He had finally reached Gillian Collins, after calling six G. Collinses in the Atlanta phone directory.

And now Leslie was on her way here.

"But don't tell her I told you. She wanted to surprise you," Gillian warned. "I'm not good at keeping secrets," she confided.

Connor's low chuckle rumbled through the phone line. "I promise. You've made me a very happy man."

"I thought so," she said airily.

"Can you do something else for me?"

"I never make rash promises," she said, following it by a yes.

The chuckle came again. Gillian found herself suddenly enchanted.

"The number where young Robin is staying. I would like tae talk tae her."

"That's easy," Gillian said. In a moment she had thumbed through the notes on her desk and given it to him.

"Thanks for everything, Gillian," he said. "Especially for Leslie."

Gillian hesitated a moment, then added, "Robin's a really good kid, but she and Leslie are very close. I can imagine a little jealousy there in the beginning."

Connor thanked her and, after cutting the connection, slowly dialed the new number and asked for Robin.

"Hello?"

"Robin?"

There was a surprised pause. "Connor?"

"Aye. I need your help," he said when she came on.

There was another pause. "I don't think you need any," Robin said finally, and Connor detected the slightest note of mischief. She knew, of course, that Leslie was on her way, and she also knew that Connor wasn't supposed to know.

"Ah, but I think I do," he said. "I wanted tae ask your permission tae propose tae your mother."

"You really love her, don't you?"

Robin's directness startled him, though he supposed it shouldn't. She had always been frank and open. It was one of the things he really liked about her.

"Aye. Does that bother you?"

"It did for a while . . . and then . . ."

Connor was silent, letting her sort out her own thoughts.

"She's been . . . really . . . quiet this week."

"Robin?"

Connor could hear Robin's even breathing over the phone as she waited for him to continue.

"I won't ask her if you can't be happy with it. Because if you're not, she won't be."

"Would we . . . have to move?"

"I don't know. 'Tis a lot tae discuss. But I will promise that if she does agree, we won't make any decisions withou' you."

"I want to graduate here." There was the tiniest bit of defiance, of uncertainty, in her voice.

"I know. We'll work out something."

"I've . . . never seen her as happy as she was last week," Robin said slowly. "I don't want to ruin that, but . . ."

"I know," Connor said gently. "You must feel like I'm stealing something from you. But I hope tae gi' you something in return. A friend. A very good friend."

"I've thought, sometimes, about having a stepdad," she ventured.

Connor winced. "It sounds depressing . . . like the wicked stepmother in all the fairy tales."

Robin chuckled. "I can't think of anyone who looks less like an evil stepmother."

"That's encouraging. I think."

"And I like kilts," Robin said, encouragement in her voice.

"There's a lot of them in Edinburgh."

"Is that a bribe?"

"A major one, I hope."

He felt like a young man again, being judged by a father, and it was a peculiar feeling. He might even have resented it if he didn't like Robin so much, didn't see and understand the vulnerability under that seventeen-year-old bravado. He thought about his son again, and how hard it would have been to ask Douglas to leave his own country and everything he loved for a step-parent he hardly knew. His son . . .

"What is Scotland like?"

The question startled him, and pleased him. At least she hadn't rejected him.

"Heaven for an artist," he said. "Wild mountains and cliffs, meadows filled with heather and thousand-year-old castles." He winked. "And everyone speaks like me. You wouldn't ha' tae bottle it."

"But then I couldn't make any money."

"I think you would ha' a hard time making it anywhere tae start with."

"Hmmmm," she said, disagreement obvious in her voice.

"Do you think you can live with it?"

Robin hesitated, then said, "Aye."

He chuckled. "You are going tae love Scotland. And I know Scotland will love you."

Connor didn't know when he'd been quite this expectant or exhilarated as he mounted the stage of the theater in Chicago. The lights were on the stage and the audience area dark. But he knew she was there. He sensed it.

Somewhere in the darkened room was Leslie, with the hair that shone like polished copper and green eyes that misted like the mountains of home and sparked like sun reflecting against a sea.

Waves of longing attacked him, and he changed the program he had planned, starting instead with a fast, witty tune that involved the audience in the chorus. He then went into Scottish favorites, the "Skye Boat Song" and "Scots Wha Hae," and finally the ballads, the plaintive sad songs of lost love.

It was time for requests. The lights now flickered over the audience, and he saw her, and it was all he could do to stay on the stage and not go down to her. She looked lovely, a soft smile on her face, her auburn hair feathering around the calm, serene features he loved.

There were several requests, including "Annie Laurie," and the song came easier than it had the other night. It was wistful and tender, and also a good-bye. He watched Leslie's face, saw the surprise and then dawning understanding, and finally a smile.

She made her own request then: "These Are My Mountains."

A wild joy filled him. She *was* giving him an answer.

He stilled his guitar and spoke into the microphone. "Tae the lady who I hope will soon share these mountains wi' me as my wife."

He didn't pay attention to the heads that turned toward Leslie, or the smiles. His fingers were strumming the guitar, and he was singing a love song to Leslie, the offer of his life as well as his mountains.

Connor played several other requests, and then finished with the "American Trilogy," a particular favorite of American audiences that combined "Dixie," "Battle Hymn of the Republic," and "Hush, Little Baby."

The audience was standing as he finished, and he played two encores, then bowed low and flashed his grin. "I've yet tae hear an answer from my lady . . . I hope you will understand."

There was a new explosion of applause, and Connor knew the private Leslie was probably flushing, but he couldn't stop the exuberant words. He wanted to be with her, and he wanted to share his pleasure with the people who liked his music.

He jumped off the stage and made his way to her, one hand on the guitar and the other grabbing her. The people separated, allowing him to make his way, join Leslie and leave as another round of applause followed them.

• • •

Leslie felt propelled by a force mightier than any she'd ever known.

Connor's hand was firm and unyielding as he led her through the crowd with more speed than she'd believed possible. Just outside the door he leaned down and kissed her, oblivious to fascinated eyes around them.

She became oblivious very quickly too.

His lips were still warm, so demanding. There was an urgency and need in them that echoed her own, an urgency and need she knew now were not temporary or fragile.

He had become so much of her life in such a short time: The rakish smile and blue eyes, the distinctive accent and deep voice, the way he cherished music and words, and the openness he had with Robin. She realized that the things she feared the most were what she loved the most. And with that knowledge the fear went away.

She surrendered the last reservation. He felt too good, too right.

The kiss deepened, right then in the hall with a growing audience, and Leslie didn't give a fig. The sense of freedom of release made her giggle suddenly. Fig, fig leaf, kilt. A natural progression of thought.

She giggled, a sound that started in her throat and moved up to make her lips quake under Connor's.

His head moved slightly, his lips surrendering their hold as he looked at her curiously.

"I'm just thinking about what Scots wear under their kilts," she said, humor bubbling in her voice.

He grinned and whispered in her ear "Everyone in the world will know soon if we don't get tae my room. All the mystery will be gone, and Scots everywhere will curse my name."

She looked up. "I love you."

Connor closed his eyes, savoring the joy that ran through him. He hadn't expected this, not yet. But he treasured the sound of the words.

"I love you, Leslie."

There was another round of clapping, and Leslie laughed, too delighted to be embarrassed.

"Then the answer is yes? Robin approves," he added hastily.

"I know," Leslie said. "I talked to her earlier today. She's decided she likes kilts too. Lots of them."

"Is that the only reason you said yes? Robin's approval?" Connor's amused voice contradicted the wry twist of his mouth.

She grinned wickedly at him. "If you want me to tell you, I think we'd better continue this conversation elsewhere."

Connor looked around at the avid onlookers, grinned, and bowed. "Thank you all for your assistance." Once more he took her hand and headed for the exit.

They didn't come up for air during the ten-minute ride to his hotel. Their lips seemed permanently attached, the fervor between them growing with each passing minute. His hands were greedy, moving inch by inch along her back, up to her neck. Touching. Loving.

The cabdriver had to clear his throat several times before they realized they'd arrived, and even then Leslie didn't want to move away from Connor's arms.

She watched as he paid the cabdriver, heard the exclamation of approval at the size of the tip, and then they were out of the taxi, and the doorman was opening the door. The lobby seemed very long, the elevator ride even longer. Finally they reached a door, and Connor unlocked it. They were inside.

Leslie turned and looked up at him, knowing her eyes expressed the deep feelings of her heart.

He brushed her lips with his. "Will you marry me, love?"

"I might as well," she said. "I can't work anymore. I've become totally useless."

He feigned disappointment, but the side of his mouth twitched with hidden laughter. "Not the enthusiasm I'd hoped for."

She arched an eyebrow at him. "You did it, you know. Those darn tapes. They just kept playing themselves over and over again. I even missed an important appointment, and I didn't even care." Her voice was accusing. Outraged.

"God bless tapes," he said as he nibbled on her ear.

"Hmmmm," Leslie agreed with mock reluctance. Her pulse speeded up and her heart skipped in crazy, expectant patterns. How did she ever think she could stay away from him?

He groaned. "I missed you so much." His lips trailed along her face and finally reached her mouth, his tongue gently touching, caressing, exploring.

Remembering.

Savoring.

Leslie relished every moment, knowing they both were making up for the past desolate week. So many lost moments, so much wasted time.

His lips moved from her mouth up to her eyes, framing them with kisses until Leslie thought she could stand no more. Yet they had to talk.

She tilted her head up. "There're so many things we have to work out."

Connor leaned down and his lips touched her forehead. "I know. I've been thinking . . ."

"Me too."

"Perhaps . . ."

"Maybe . . ."

The words came out together, and both stopped speaking. They just stared at each other instead, as if the other would disappear in a wisp of smoke.

"I've missed you, lass."

In response Leslie stretched upward and kissed him wistfully, longingly, and then neither needed more words. Leslie moved into the planes and angles of his body. She felt his arousal under his kilt, and naked desire rushed through her, joining waves of warm emotion, of love, of tenderness. Talk, she suddenly realized, could wait. Would have to wait.

Her face pressed against his chest, listening to the beat of his heart—the heart that had prompted him to come after her, the heart that showed itself in every touch of his hands. She moved back to look straight up into his eyes, and her hands entangled themselves in his hair. Her lips reached up again to meet his, and the whisper-soft touch turned stormy, full of electricity and thunder and sensation.

Their eyes feasted on each other, as if it had been years rather than days since they last met. Connor's tongue eagerly sought the softness of her mouth, each sweet, sensitive part, and teased and explored until he felt her body tremble, and then he picked her up and carried her to the bed.

Leslie felt her body stiffen with anticipation, with physical and emotional need of him. She wanted to give him joy and get joy in return. She wanted to give and take with a ferocity that frightened her.

He put her down on the bed and sat next to her, and she felt that incredible sense of belonging and warmth that she'd found only with him.

His hands undid the buttons of her dress, and then slowly, sensuously, slid down the pair of panty hose she wore. He started to take off his shirt, but she stopped him.

"Let me," she said, and she did as he had, tracing her hands against his heated skin as she slid the vest from his arms and then untied the lace on his shirt, slipping the shirt over his head. Finally there was the heavy belt, and she needed his help for the fastenings of the kilt.

She marveled at the perfection of his body, and she marveled at her own boldness. But he had done that to her, had awakened her to her own sensuality and showed her it was a fine thing. Fine and natural.

Leslie had little time to wonder about such things though. His mouth was on her breasts, first one and then the other, and his hands were tracing intricate trails of fire on her body until she thought she would explode.

She drew him near to her, loving the knowledge that this time they had all night and more, and they could explore each other, each nook and plane, and she planned to do exactly that.

She heard him gasp as her fingers kneaded the back of his neck and felt his lean hips move about her. Her body arched up toward him as a deep, pulsating need overtook every other emotion. She wanted him to be a part of her, to become one with her, and her arms tightened around him, drawing him deeper and deeper, rejoicing in each strong thrust that brought her closer and closer to the core of her body.

The exquisite, tantalizing pleasure climbed and climbed, finally erupting into a shattering explosion of sensations. Two climaxed as one, their cries one cry.

For moments they lay like that together, their bodies trembling from the aftershocks of their lovemaking, his lips brushing her mouth, then her cheek, with such tenderness, Leslie felt tears gather in her eyes.

Neither spoke. For a time it was enough to feel

each other's essence, the damp skin, the beat of accelerated hearts, the soft brush of air in the sighs of sated pleasure.

But then Leslie wanted even more. Her tongue trailed along his chest, taking an occasional gentle nip. She felt a savageness she'd never felt before, a tender savageness that wanted to consume, that wanted to take and take, demand and demand, give and give.

All the fear of commitment was gone, and she wanted everything there was to have. Like a newly liberated bird, she wanted to fly and soar and taste the wind and the headiness of freedom.

She laughed with the joy of it, and Connor joined her, feeling her exultation. They rolled over and over on the bed, laughing and exploring the sensations of movement, one against the other, until their bodies arched together again and in a soul-shattering journey climbed beyond the limits of experience or even imagination.

They clung to each other, whispering words of love, laughing with the pure joy of being alive, of being together. They drowsed together, occasionally stirring to drop a kiss on the closest available place of the other, hands kneading at times, touching in wonder at others, both aware in some sleepy place of a profound sense of belonging and deep, deep bliss.

They awoke as the first rays of morning sun entered the room, and they showered together.

Leslie had never showered with a man before. She had been shy with her husband—young and shy and then even a bit afraid of him, of his roughness.

But now when Connor stood naked and led her to the bathroom and the shower, she followed easily. They soaped each other and kissed in the full force of the spray, rinsed each other, and kissed again, feeling the warm water tumbling over them. They must have kissed for a very long time, for then they felt the water turning cold, and they giggled like children as icy splinters fell on them.

There was nothing to do but get warm again. In the fastest, most pleasurable way.

It was midmorning before Connor ordered room service. When breakfast came, they lay contentedly in bed eating, at times feeding each other and nibbling crumbs from each other's lips. Leslie thought this was intimacy at its very finest . . . well, almost finest.

To Connor, the last day and night seemed like a miracle, so spontaneous and giving and joyful. Tenderness swelled in him like a great tidal wave. There would be so many other days like this, nights such as they had just spent. New feelings, new adventures, new explorations. Only now did he realize how dull the past had been. He had enjoyed life because it was in his nature to enjoy life, but he'd never had these glorious highs, this intensity of feeling that made the world glow with a special brightness.

He finished eating a section of grapefruit she'd plunged in his mouth. "Enough," he commanded. He carefully put down the tray. "Are you going tae make me get down on my knees?"

She looked at him silently.

"You've still not answered my question," he said. "Even after I've already received permission from your closest relative."

"I thought I told you in other ways," she said softly.

"Ah, but I'm a direct Scot," he said.

"Then I'll give my direct Scot a direct answer— Yes."

He grinned. "No ifs, buts, or maybes?"

There had been lots of those yesterday. But last night was a time of give-and-take, of partnership, of sharing. Leslie had no more fears of loss. He was opening her world, not narrowing it.

"No," she said softly, and knew from the look in his eyes that she'd just given him a very rich gift.

Connor leaned over and kissed her . . . a touch so full of promise that her heart nearly shattered with it.

And then he took her hand, pulling her against his broad chest.

"I've been thinking . . ."

"Connor . . ."

The words came simultaneously.

Leslie kissed his chest in an impulsive, irrepressible gesture.

"Lass, if you keep doing tha', I'll not be responsible for my own actions."

"I stopped being that days ago," Leslie said, with a certain smug satisfaction.

She looked so self-satisfied, Connor had to kiss her. At this rate, he knew, they would never get anything accomplished. Outside of the obvious.

But he knew it was time to discuss the problems. They wouldn't go away. And the one thing he knew he had in common with Leslie was that he liked things settled. So he tried to straighten his face, but, he was afraid, failed miserably. He feared he had a perpetually silly grin on his face.

"Leslie," he tried again, but the mere sound of her name softened his voice and made it a song.

"Hmmmm, I love you," she said, nibbling at his ear.

"And now we must decide what tae do about it," he said in mock severity.

"I know," she replied, reluctantly letting go of his earlobe. "I've been thinking too."

"We can spend half a year in Scotland and the other half here," he hurried on. "We can spend spring and summer there, and Robin can stay with us over the summer. We can come back tae the States in fall and winter, and I can tour, using Atlanta as a home base. Tha' way, you and Robin will be apart only three months, and she'll be in college then."

Leslie stared at him. She'd been ready to go to Scotland with him. She'd talked to Robin about it yesterday, and though Robin wasn't one hundred percent enthusiastic about leaving Atlanta and her friends, she'd agreed to it.

"And," he added, "you can open an Edinburgh branch of your company. There's many a Scots performer who tours, and you and Gillian are very guid with us Scots."

The *r* in "very" rolled like a drum in the room, and Leslie chuckled. "With one Scot," she corrected.

He took a moment to look pleased at her comment, then continued, "And there're Scottish festivals, and with computers and faxes, you ca' work taegether on other projects. Gillian thought it was a fine idea."

Gillian would, Leslie thought drolly, but still her heart wanted to burst right then and there. She had painfully made her choice in the past few days, and she'd thought it meant giving up something very, very important to her. And now he was offering to give up something important to him, months in his beloved Scotland. She knew his American performances usually lasted only three or four months, but he was willing to spend six months here. For her. For her and Robin.

That's what love was about, she suddenly knew. Compromises. Giving. Sharing.

She was silent for so long that Connor was suddenly afraid. Perhaps she didn't agree.

"I know Robin has tae finish school," he said. "And it's best tae do it here. If you'll marry me now, I ca' stay in the States till after the yule holidays, then I ha' tae go back tae Scotland for some recordings. You and Robin ca' join me for the spring holidays, and then in the summer you can move there wi' me."

Leslie heard the heavy brogue, the brogue especially distinctive because of his emotions, because of an uncertainty that she knew was rare. Uncertainty because he wanted to make her happy, and had worked out the best plan he could. She loved that uncertainty. She loved him for thinking about what was best for Robin. She loved him for being him, for being so caring and loving and thoughtful. She loved . . . so many things. The blue of his eyes, the smile that lit his face, the body that fit so well in hers. She loved his warmth and his laughter and his songs. She loved the way he made her feel. So complete. So utterly complete.

And she would have done anything to be with him.

She nodded. "I think it sounds wonderful."

His arms went around her, pulling her tightly to him. "When would you like tae marry?"

Today. Now. But she had to think of Robin, and Gillian, and others. But particularly Robin. "Thanksgiving?" she said. "Four weeks."

He hesitated, aware of the American holiday but not quite sure of the date.

Leslie gave it to him, and Connor mentally ran over his schedule. He would be performing in San Francisco for two weeks, but not on that Thursday. They could marry on Thanksgiving, and he could take her to San Francisco. Perhaps Robin, too, for a few days, and then he and Leslie could take a wedding trip up the Coast to Portland, where his next engagement was.

"It's much tae long," he grumbled, "but 'twill have tae do."

"Just enough time for me to learn how to take

off kilts," Leslie teased. "Although the one nice thing about kilts . . ."

"We Scots are foresighted."

"And thrifty."

"Aye, that tae."

"And fierce."

"Aye," he agreed again, "passionately so."

"Aye," she teased playfully, and the sultry way she said the word invited him to show her just how much.

Later, they called Robin together to tell her their plans, and Leslie asked her to be her maid of honor.

After Robin said yes, Connor gave Leslie a moment of privacy with her daughter, saying he needed to get something downstairs. It was only another way he showed his understanding, and Leslie thought how very lucky she was, before she turned back to the phone.

"Are you sure, Robin?"

Robin paused. "I wasn't in the beginning, but . . . he's special, Mom. I don't think I want you to lose him."

Pleasure flooded Leslie.

"How long are you going to stay?" Robin asked.

Leslie truly didn't know. She had responsibilities, but she felt she had just found Connor. She had been too cautious before, afraid of the implications, and now she had all of him and didn't want to let him go. Not so soon, even knowing that in four weeks they would be together again.

"Denise's mother said I could stay all week," Robin offered, and Leslie wondered what things had come to when a teenage daughter urged her mother to spend an illicit week with a man.

"I mean, you're going to be married in a month," Robin said in a disgusted voice, as if she read her mother's mind. All too many people were doing that these days, Leslie thought. Connor, Gilly, and now Robin. Good old private Leslie was private no longer.

What a wonderful feeling!

"A week then," she told Robin.

"Should I call Aunt Gilly?" Robin said.

Leslie hesitated a moment, then chuckled to herself. "Yeah," she said, imitating her daughter's favorite form of assent.

When Connor returned, this time with a bucket of ice and a bottle of champagne, she pulled him down next to her. "Would you like me for a week?"

He kissed the tip of her nose. "I canna think of anything better, but . . . your business?"

Leslie giggled. "I have one big project, and I think Gilly can take care of it."

Connor looked at the face flushed and full of humor. "You're thinking of something."

"Gilly can't stand my client."

"And . . ."

"Well, I wasn't too eager to meet you."

"And . . ." His voice was patient but persistent.

"And look what happened." Leslie's voice was triumphant.

He chuckled. "Now you don't think lightning strikes twice?"

"Is it lightning?"

"Something God sent," he whispered as he nuzzled her neck.

And then they both forgot about Gillian and Atlanta and Scotland and business.

They had something better to do.

THE EDITOR'S CORNER

Next month LOVESWEPT presents an Easter parade of six fabulous romances. Not even April showers can douse the terrific mood you'll be in after reading each and every one of these treasures.

The hero of Susan Connell's new LOVESWEPT, #606, is truly **SOME KIND OF WONDERFUL.** As mysterious and exciting as the Greek islands he calls home, Alex Stoner is like a gorgeous god whose mouth promises pagan pleasures. He's also a cool businessman who never lets a woman get close. But prim and proper Sandy Patterson, widow of his college roommate, is unlike any he's ever known, and he sets out to make her ache for his own brand of passion. Susan takes you on a roller coaster of emotion with this romance.

Kay Hooper continues her MEN OF MYSTERIES PAST series with **HUNTING THE WOLFE,** LOVESWEPT #607. Security expert Wolfe Nickerson appeared in the first book in the series, **THE TOUCH OF MAX,** LOVESWEPT #595, and in this new novel, he almost finds himself bested by a pint-sized computer programmer. Storm Tremaine blows into his life like a force of nature, promising him the chase of his life . . . and hinting she's fast enough to catch him! When he surrenders to her womanly charms, he doesn't know that Storm holds a secret . . . a secret that could forever destroy his trust. Kay is at her best with this terrific love story.

BREATHLESS, LOVESWEPT #608 by Diane Pershing, is how Hollis Blake feels when Tony Stellini walks into her gift shop. The tall, dark, and sensuous lawyer makes the air sizzle with his wildfire energy, and for the first time Hollis longs to taste every pleasure she's never had, pursue all the dreams she's been denied. Her innocence stirs an overpowering desire in Tony, but he senses that with this untouched beauty, he has to take it one slow, delicious step at a time. This is a romance to relish, a treat from Diane.

Linda Cajio begins **DANCING IN THE DARK,** LOVESWEPT #609, with an eye-opening scene in which the hero is engaged in a sacred ceremony and dancing naked in the woods! Jake Halford feels a little silly performing the men's movement ritual, but Charity Brown feels downright embarrassed at catching him at it. How can she ever work with her company's new vice president without remembering the thrilling sight of his muscles and power? The way Linda has these two learning how to mix business and pleasure is a pure delight.

HANNAH'S HUNK, LOVESWEPT #610 by Sandra Chastain, is nothing less than a sexy rebel with a southern drawl . . . and an ex-con whom Hannah Clendening "kidnaps" so he could pose for the cover of her Fantasy Romance. Dan Bailey agrees, but only if Hannah plays the heroine and he gets to kiss her. When desire flares between them like a force field, neither believes that what they feel could last. Of course Sandra, with her usual wit and charm, makes sure there's a happily ever after for this unusual couple.

Finally, there's **THE TROUBLE WITH MAGIC,** LOVESWEPT #611 by Mary Kay McComas. Harriet Wheaton has an outrageous plan to keep Payton Dunsmore from foreclosing on the great manor house on Jovette Island. Marooning them there, she tells him that she's trying to fulfill the old legend of enemies meeting on Jovette and falling in love! Payton's furious at first, but he soon succumbs to the enchantment of the island . . . and Harriet herself. Mary Kay delivers pure magic with this marvelous romance.

On sale this month from FANFARE are four outstanding novels. If you missed **TEMPERATURES RISING** by blockbuster author Sandra Brown when it first came out, now's your chance to grab a copy of this wonderfully evocative love story. Chantal duPont tells herself that she needs Scout Ritland only to build a much-needed bridge on the South Pacific island she calls home. And when the time comes for him to leave, she must make the painful decision of letting him go—or risking everything by taking a chance on love.

From beloved author Rosanne Bittner comes **OUTLAW HEARTS,** a stirring new novel of heart-stopping danger and burning desire. At twenty, Miranda Hayes has known more than her share of heartache and loss. Then she clashes with the notorious gunslinger Jake Harkner, a hard-hearted loner with a price on his head, and finds within herself a deep well of courage . . . and feelings of desire she's never known before.

Fanfare is proud to publish **THE LAST HIGHWAYMAN,** the first historical romance by Katherine O'Neal, a truly exciting new voice in women's fiction. In this delectable action-packed novel, Christina has money, power, and position, but she has never known reckless passion, never found enduring love . . . until she is kidnapped by a dangerously handsome bandit who needs her to heal his tormented soul.

In the bestselling tradition of Danielle Steel, **CONFIDENCES** by Penny Hayden is a warm, deeply moving novel about four "thirty-something" mothers whose lives are interwoven by a long-held secret—a secret that could now save the life of a seventeen-year-old boy dying of leukemia.

Also available now in the hardcover edition from Doubleday is **MASK OF NIGHT** by Lois Wolfe, a stunning historical novel of romantic suspense. When an actress and a cattle rancher join forces against a diabolical villain, the result is an unforgettable story of love and vengeance.

Happy reading!

With warmest wishes,

Nita Taublib

Nita Taublib
Associate Publisher
LOVESWEPT and FANFARE

OFFICIAL RULES TO WINNERS CLASSIC SWEEPSTAKES

No Purchase necessary. To enter the sweepstakes follow instructions found elsewhere in this offer. You can also enter the sweepstakes by hand printing your name, address, city, state and zip code on a 3" x 5" piece of paper and mailing it to: Winners Classic Sweepstakes, P.O. Box 785, Gibbstown, NJ 08027. Mail each entry separately. Sweepstakes begins 12/1/91. Entries must be received by 6/1/93. Some presentations of this sweepstakes may feature a deadline for the Early Bird prize. If the offer you receive does, then to be eligible for the Early Bird prize your entry must be received according to the Early Bird date specified. Not responsible for lost, late, damaged, misdirected, illegible or postage due mail. Mechanically reproduced entries are not eligible. All entries become property of the sponsor and will not be returned.

Prize Selection/Validations: Winners will be selected in random drawings on or about 7/30/93, by VENTURA ASSOCIATES, INC., an independent judging organization whose decisions are final. Odds of winning are determined by total number of entries received. Circulation of this sweepstakes is estimated not to exceed 200 million. Entrants need not be present to win. All prizes are guaranteed to be awarded and delivered to winners. Winners will be notified by mail and may be required to complete an affidavit of eligibility and release of liability which must be returned within 14 days of date of notification or alternate winners will be selected. Any guest of a trip winner will also be required to execute a release of liability. Any prize notification letter or any prize returned to a participating sponsor, Bantam Doubleday Dell Publishing Group, Inc., its participating divisions or subsidiaries, or VENTURA ASSOCIATES, INC. as undeliverable will be awarded to an alternate winner. Prizes are not transferable. No multiple prize winners except as may be necessary due to unavailability, in which case a prize of equal or greater value will be awarded. Prizes will be awarded approximately 90 days after the drawing. All taxes, automobile license and registration fees, if applicable, are the sole responsibility of the winners. Entry constitutes permission (except where prohibited) to use winners' names and likenesses for publicity purposes without further or other compensation.

Participation: This sweepstakes is open to residents of the United States and Canada, except for the province of Quebec. This sweepstakes is sponsored by Bantam Doubleday Dell Publishing Group, Inc. (BDD), 666 Fifth Avenue, New York, NY 10103. Versions of this sweepstakes with different graphics will be offered in conjunction with various solicitations or promotions by different subsidiaries and divisions of BDD. Employees and their families of BDD, its division, subsidiaries, advertising agencies, and VENTURA ASSOCIATES, INC., are not eligible.

Canadian residents, in order to win, must first correctly answer a time limited arithmetical skill testing question. Void in Quebec and wherever prohibited or restricted by law. Subject to all federal, state, local and provincial laws and regulations.

Prizes: The following values for prizes are determined by the manufacturers' suggested retail prices or by what these items are currently known to be selling for at the time this offer was published. Approximate retail values include handling and delivery of prizes. Estimated maximum retail value of prizes: 1 Grand Prize ($27,500 if merchandise or $25,000 Cash); 1 First Prize ($3,000); 5 Second Prizes ($400 each); 35 Third Prizes ($100 each); 1,000 Fourth Prizes ($9.00 each); 1 Early Bird Prize ($5,000); Total approximate maximum retail value is $50,000. Winners will have the option of selecting any prize offered at level won. Automobile winner must have a valid driver's license at the time the car is awarded. Trips are subject to space and departure availability. Certain black-out dates may apply. Travel must be completed within one year from the time the prize is awarded. Minors must be accompanied by an adult. Prizes won by minors will be awarded in the name of parent or legal guardian.

For a list of Major Prize Winners (available after 7/30/93): send a self-addressed, stamped envelope entirely separate from your entry to: Winners Classic Sweepstakes Winners, P.O. Box 825, Gibbstown, NJ 08027. Requests must be received by 6/1/93. DO NOT SEND ANY OTHER CORRESPONDENCE TO THIS P.O. BOX.

Women's Fiction

On Sale in February

TEMPERATURES RISING

56045-X $5.99/6.99 in Canada
☐ **by Sandra Brown**

New York Times bestselling author of
A WHOLE NEW LIGHT and FRENCH SILK

A contemporary tale of love and passion in the South Pacific.

OUTLAW HEARTS

29807-0 $5.99/6.99 in Canada
☐ **by Rosanne Bittner**

Bestselling author of SONG OF THE WOLF,
praised by *Romantic Times* as "a stunning
achievement...that moves the soul and fills the heart."

THE LAST HIGHWAYMAN

56065-4 $5.50/6.50 in Canada
☐ **by Katherine O'Neal**

Fascinating historical fact and sizzling romantic fiction meet
in this sensual tale of a legendary bandit and a scandalous
high-born lady.

CONFIDENCES

56170-7 $4.99/5.99 in Canada
☐ **by Penny Hayden**

"Thirtysomething" meets Danielle Steel—four best friends
are bound by an explosive secret.

Women's Fiction

On Sale in March

ONCE AN ANGEL

☐   29409-1 $5.50/6.50 in Canada

by Teresa Medeiros

Bestselling author of HEATHER AND VELVET

A captivating historical romance that sweeps from the wilds of an exotic paradise to the elegance of Victorian England.
"Teresa Medeiros writes rare love stories to cherish."
— <u>Romantic Times</u>

IN A ROGUE'S ARMS

☐   29692-2 $4.99/5.99 in Canada

by Virginia Brown writing as Virginia Lynn

Author of LYON'S PRIZE

A passion-filled retelling of the beloved Robin Hood tale, set in Texas of the 1870's. The first of Bantam's new "Once Upon a Time" romances: passionate historical romances with themes from fairy tales, myths, and legends.

THE LADY AND THE CHAMP

☐   29655-8 $4.99/5.99 in Canada

by Fran Baker

Bestselling Loveswept author Fran Baker's first mainstream romance! The passionate story of a boxer/lawyer and the interior decorator who inherited his gym — and won his heart.
"Unforgettable...a warm, wonderful knockout of a book."
— Julie Garwood